Good,
Bad & Sexy

JENNIFER LYON

WRITING AS JENNIFER APODACA

Good, Bad & Sexy
Copyright © 2017 Jennifer Apodaca
All rights reserved.

Cover Design: Jaycee DeLorenzo of Sweet 'N Spicy Designs
Copy Editor: http://www.kimberlycannoneditor.com
Formatted by: Author E.M.S.

Published by Jennifer Lyon Books
www.jenniferlyonbooks.com

Originally Published by Kensington Publishing Corp. in
2007 in the Sun, Sand, Sex Anthology.
Original Title: You Give Love a Good Name

ISBN: 978-0-9967169-9-4

Published in the United States of America.

Blazing hot, that is how Nick and Lexie are together. This story is a scorcher and one that every reader will eat up. —*Coffee Time Romance*

Chapter 1

Four months earlier

LEXIE ROLLINS BACKED UP AS the bride threw the bouquet, trying to stay out of range.

She stopped short when her shoulders hit a hard male chest. She jerked in reaction and nearly lost her balance. Large, warm hands settled on her bare arms to steady her. From behind her, a low voice chuckled and said, "Ducking the bouquet? I thought you women were supposed to fight for it?"

Recognizing the voice of the bride's brother, Nick Vardolous, she enjoyed the feel of his hands on her arms for a few seconds. It was just a little indulgence, perfectly innocent, she told herself. Then she turned, sliding out of his touch, and smiled up at him. "The wedding planner doesn't catch the bouquet." He stood beneath one of the crystal chandeliers in his dark suit and Lexie was struck by how good-looking he was. He had that hot Greek thing going on from his wavy black hair all the way down his six-foot frame. Strong bone structure showed off his incredible eyes, so light green that they sometimes took on a gold hue. Every time she looked into his eyes, she felt a little shock of lust jolt her system.

"You deserve more than a bouquet for putting up with my sister and mom."

She laughed. "It's my job. I get paid to handle the problems in weddings." The truth was she hated it, but she was stuck until her mom fully recovered from her heart attack and came back to work. She tore her gaze from Nick to look around and make sure everything was in order. "The bride and groom are leaving. I need to—"

He touched her hand.

The words locked in her throat as attraction tingled up her arm and down her spine. They'd flirted for days. She really liked Nick, but he was the client's brother, not a date.

His gaze turned intense. "We'll talk later." He gently squeezed her hand, then strode away to hug his sister and shake hands with his new brother-in-law.

Lexie watched for a moment, surprised that in just a few days Nick had stirred a sexual longing in her. He made her think of hot sultry nights, sweaty skin and frantic need. Thick desire pooled low in her belly. What was it about him? He wasn't her usual type. She liked safe and secure, while Nick was anything but. She didn't know what he did for a career or where he lived. He had an air of mystery and danger, while she was boring and dependable. She shook it off, determined to finish her job.

An hour later she picked up the last box off the table, turned, and almost yelped. "Hey, Nick, I didn't hear you." She'd seen him talking to his family as they were all leaving, and had assumed he'd go with them. He must have really meant it about wanting to talk later. But about what?

Nick reached out and took the heavy box from her. "You finished in here?"

She headed out the door to the parking lot. "Yep. Your sister is officially married and off on her honeymoon, the hall is cleaned up, and everyone lived through the experience." She stopped at her light blue Explorer and opened the rear door.

Nick slid the box in.

She smiled at him. "Thanks. I guess you're heading back to...wherever you came from?" Nick had told her his job kept him traveling, but he hadn't been specific about what his job was.

He shut the rear door and turned to look at her beneath the parking lot lights. "Leaving in the morning."

Nodding, she said, "It's been nice to see you these last couple days. And thanks for carrying the box." She wondered if he really wanted to talk to her or if he had just used her as an excuse to avoid his family.

"Lexie."

His voice was soft and low, the kind of tone that made a woman pay attention. "Yes?"

"Spend the night with me."

Her eyes widened. "Uh, the night?" *Stupid!* She

knew what he meant. But she didn't do stuff like that.

Nick stood a couple feet away, watching her. "You're a sexy woman and I'm interested in you. I'm leaving early in the morning, but I can promise you an unforgettable night."

He was so incredibly honest, and he stayed a respectful distance away. She liked that. She liked him. She wanted him, but she didn't do one-night stands. She was so tempted, but no. "I can't, but thanks for, uh..." She felt like an idiot and looked down at the black pavement. *Thanks? Thanks for wanting to have sex with me?* God.

"Lexie."

That was some voice he had. Repressing a sigh, she looked up. "No." She hurried around him to the driver's side, fumbling with her key to unlock the door.

Nick slid the keys from her clumsy fingers and clicked the unlock button.

Hot embarrassment crawled up her neck, but she forced herself to turn and face him. "I'm sorry, I just..."

He smiled down at her. "I know what the word *no* means. Relax. I'm just going to make sure you get in your car and lock the door. It's a habit from having a baby sister."

God, she wanted to be someone else, the kind of woman who went home with a sexy man who made her feel desired and wild, while at the same time looking out for her safety. He probably got women to go home with him all the time. That thought made her feel even worse somehow. She blurted out, "I'm not impulsive."

He opened the driver's side door.

She slipped past him and hoped the flush crawling up her neck and face didn't show. Holding her skirt, she climbed up to the driver's seat, bringing her eye to eye with Nick.

He handed her the keys.

"Thanks."

"Lexie."

He had to stop saying her name like that. It was seductive, wickedly melting her common sense until all she wanted to do was crawl into his arms. She tried to keep her gaze focused out the front window of the SUV, but against her will she turned to look at him. "Nick."

"If I were another guy…"

He was trying to make her feel better. "But you're not."

"No, I don't hang around in relationships. I'm a loner. But if I were looking for a relationship, I'd work hard to get you interested in me."

He was seducing her with what ifs, or maybe it was his honesty. "And if I were an impulsive woman…"

His smile reached his eyes. "I'd be a lucky son of a bitch."

She laughed. Nick was sexy, so easy to be around.

Something flared in his green-gold gaze. Then he leaned forward and said, "Ah, damn, Lexie. I'm not going to be able to close this door until I kiss you."

He put his hand on her shoulder, then slid his fingers up to cup the back of her head.

Warm excitement pooled in her stomach, and her muscles softened in reaction. Nick leaned forward and kissed her. The touch of his mouth sent sensual shivers down her spine to curl deep inside her. His hot breath tasted like wine from all the toasts. Putting her hand on his arm, she felt the hard ridges of his muscles.

Felt the pulse of both their excitement.

Nick shifted just enough and she opened her mouth, wanting him inside her. Wanting to feel the rush as his tongue touched hers.

Nick pulled back, breathing hard, and his green eyes warmed to a light gold tone. "Time for you to go home, wedding planner."

"But..."

He shook his head. Determination hardened his features and his mouth lost the curve of amusement. "I'm not the sticking kind, and you're not a one-nighter. Go." He stepped back and shut the door.

He was still standing there when she drove away.

Present day

She had to find a way to keep the hostages alive...

Lexie Rollins stopped typing. How was she going to get her heroine and the hostages out alive? Her laptop was getting warm on her bare thighs. She shut it down and stood up on the patio off her room that overlooked the ocean.

She'd recommended this place for months as a perfect honeymoon for the clients of My Perfect Wedding. Sand Castle Resort in San Diego, California, lived up to its reputation.

It was beautiful, with lush tropical plants and very private Mediterranean-style rooms right on the beach. The walls of the rooms were done in textured layers of paint in a color scheme of either blue, green, or rustic browns. The rooms also had beautiful mosaic tile to match, exquisite wrought iron beds and tables, and ceiling fans to complement the air-conditioning.

Perfect for honeymoons and hiding from stalkers.

Since just the idea of a wedding made Lexie nauseous, she was there to hide from her stalker. And the media. And her lawyer. And her family.

In short, her life sucked.

But the good news was...hell, there was no good news. No, that wasn't true. She still had the memory of the face of the groom—William Harry Livingston's face when he had cornered her at the lovely garden wedding rehearsal dinner, drunker than a seaman on leave, and tried to seduce her. He had unzipped his pants and revealed Mr. Pathetic Penis to her.

Ugh. For the first time in Lexie's entire life, she'd lost it. Truly lost it. She'd grabbed up the staple gun she'd used to secure the decorations and stapled Harry's pants closed. Then she stapled his pants to his waist to prevent any further viewings of Mr. Pathetic. She told him to save it for his bride.

He cried, actually *cried*.

Lexie had chalked it up to a stressed and drunk groom and forgotten all about it.

Until she was arrested for assault and battery. With a staple gun.

Wedding Planner Goes Ballistic with Staple Gun was just one headline that resulted from the stapled groom giving interviews. Her family tried to stage an intervention to get her help. They were sure she was cracking up. And they needed her to get over it real quick and get back to work as a wedding planner.

They told her to forget all this stalker business. No one was sneaking into her apartment and booting up her laptop, she just forgot to shut it down. And everyone lost underwear at those Laundromats, no one was stealing them. In short, no one was stalking her, she was just imagining it. Like one of her plots for the thriller she was never going to write. Lexie needed to *get real* and *face reality* and *be reasonable* and *realize wedding planning is a good career.*

Even her lawyer didn't believe her.

She had no one to blame but herself. She was the one who had let family treat her like this her entire life. Determined to solve her own problems, she hired a PI to watch her apartment and discover the identity of the creep stalking her. Then she'd go back and fight these ridiculous charges.

Hopefully, her PI would catch the stalker in the

next few days. And with a little luck, a few more days away from home would help her get some perspective on her life. Standing at the balcony in the light afternoon breeze was a good way to start. The briny scent of the ocean was sharp, while the bright sun made her squint. Couples were spread out on the white sand, some sheltered by blue and white cabanas while others soaked up the sun in lounge chairs. A few people swam in the waves. Waiters moved effortlessly as they served cold drinks.

One man walking out of the waves caught her attention. Even from the distance she could see he was tall. And buff. He wore white board shorts with blue and black trim. The water made his hair look slicked back and dark.

A jolt of familiarity raced through her and she leaned forward with her hands on the railing of her balcony. His confident walk...

It was the involuntary tingle of her mouth that pried the name loose in her brain.

Nick Vardolous. The hot Greek one-kiss wonder. He'd kissed her and walked away.

What the hell was Nick doing here? She didn't believe in coincidences. Her world was too crazy, too out of control for Nick to have just shown up at the same exclusive beach resort where she was. Especially a resort that catered to couples like honeymooners. He'd made it perfectly clear that he wasn't interested in couplehood.

A disturbing thought rushed through her—what if he was another reporter tracking her? He'd said he traveled a lot for work, but she didn't know what that work was.

An even darker thought occurred to her. What if Nick was her stalker?

She didn't believe it. A man who asked straight out for what he wanted? Why would he stalk her? Nick was handsome and had good social skills; he didn't need to stalk women.

But what if he was the stalker? Wasn't Ted Bundy handsome and socially adept? Fear skittered up her spine, and she shivered in the warm afternoon breeze. The loneliness pressed down on her.

She had to find out what Nick Vardolous was doing at the resort.

After discovering that Lexie wasn't in her room, Nick charmed a maid into letting him in. This was an easy bond recovery, one that probably didn't require him to do a room search. Hell, he wasn't even hiding his presence at the resort. Lexie had no reason to be afraid of him, and he was sure she would cooperate. She had signed the bond agreement that pretty much signed away her civil rights and gave him the authority to arrest her and take her back to Santa Barbara. Since the maid assumed he got locked out and that he was knocking to get his wife to let him in, Nick seized the opportunity.

But he didn't think Lexie was running from the law. Her room didn't look like she was on the run—

no hair dye in the bathroom or other telltale signs. She had left her cell phone in the room, turned off. Her lawyer had already told him she wasn't answering her cell. She had a laptop, which he supposed she could use to look for a map to Mexico or book a flight, but he doubted it. Looking at the two paperback novels on her bedside table, the shorts, bikinis, and sundresses in the closet and dresser, he thought she'd just gone on vacation. Her lawyer admitted that he hadn't reminded her about the court date she missed.

Her lawyer and family seemed to think she had snapped. Nick doubted it. In the four days he'd seen Lexie at his sister's wedding, nothing made her lose her composure. His sister and mother had spent a lot of time with her to arrange the wedding, and both of them insisted Lexie was calm and reasonable. She herself said she wasn't impulsive. Nick suspected she just thought the whole arrest was stupid.

He sure did. Any man who claimed a woman assaulted him with a staple gun was a hard man to take seriously. Hell, Nick felt like buying the man a staple remover and telling him to get over it.

Usually he didn't take these pissant cases, but he was doing it as a favor to her lawyer, and because he didn't want some other unprofessional bounty hunter getting a hold of Lexie.

He didn't like the idea of another man touching Lexie at all. That woman had gotten under his skin. His best bet was to talk to her tonight, then pack her up first thing in the morning and get her back to Santa Barbara. Her lawyer had turned out to have some balls and probably a little guilt at not making sure she knew about the missed court date, and he'd negotiated with a sympathetic judge to get Lexie a plea agreement of anger management classes and her solemn promise to stay away from staple guns. The agreement stipulated that Lexie show up in court in five days, and if she didn't, then she would face a trial and wait it out in jail.

He'd get her there and he'd walk away. That's what Nick did best. There was nothing that caused him any concern in her room, so he left, letting the automatic lock do its job when he pulled the door closed. He walked on the brick path beneath the lush foliage toward his room. The ocean roared not far away. He thought about getting in some surfing before heading back with Lexie. He rounded the corner of the terra cotta building that held his room and stopped.

The door was propped open a sliver by something wedged in at the bottom. From the green color, he thought it might be the room-service book. He could hear the tapping sound of sandals on the tile inside his room, and the shuffling of papers. The maid didn't usually wear sandals or shuffle through paperwork.

He sighed, having a pretty good idea who it was in his room. The question was, why? He did a visual sweep of the area, but he didn't spot anyone. No lookout or any reason to think that someone he'd apprehended in the past had tracked him down for a little revenge. Quietly he walked to the door, which was set back in an arched doorway. He eased it open and stepped inside.

Lexie Rollins stood by his bed, holding the mug shot of herself. She looked up, glared at him, and demanded, "Just who the hell are you and why do you have pictures of me?"

Chapter 2

NICK WENT INTO HIS ROOM and shut the door. Lexie wore a light blue sundress short enough to show off her long, tanned legs. Jerking his gaze back up her slender, five-foot-seven-inch frame, he focused on her furious chocolate-brown eyes. Her long, silky brunette hair was pulled back in a ponytail, making her cheekbones more prominent. She might have lost a few pounds, but she was even more pretty and enticing than he remembered. It almost made him forget that he was there as a fugitive recovery agent, not a lover.

He shook it off and moved toward her. Then he saw the tremble in her hand holding the picture. That brought him to a stop halfway to the bed where she had the stuff spread out. He knew she was angry, but scared? Was she afraid of him? "Lexie, I can explain."

She dropped her gaze to the mug shot the police took the night they'd arrested her. Then she looked up. "Is it you?"

"What?" He didn't have a clue what she was talking about.

She took a breath, forcibly calming herself. "Why are you here? And don't lie."

It bothered him that she didn't trust him. "I've never lied to you."

"Yeah, well, you didn't tell me a whole hell of a lot about yourself, either."

True. He didn't talk about his job with women he was interested in. He kept his life separate. What bothered him was the edgy fear in Lexie's voice. He decided the best thing to do was to be straight. Now that Lexie was a job, sex was out of the question. So he told her the truth. "I'm a bounty hunter. Your lawyer pulled some strings and got me hired to bring you back to appear in court in five days. He's negotiated a good deal for you."

She stilled like a statue. "A bounty hunter? They're paying you to bring me in? I'm a job?"

What did she expect? Nick couldn't help but look at her full mouth and remember that kiss. It had taken all his will to send her home that night. He'd wanted her, but that kiss was too hot, the chemistry between them too volatile; there was just too much emotion there. And Lexie was too much of a one-man woman. If he'd taken her back to his hotel, then walked out in the morning, she'd have been left hurt.

And he'd have felt like a jerk. So he did the right thing.

Now she looked hurt anyway. Or was that skeptical? Maybe she didn't believe him. "I'm doing you a favor," he said gruffly. "Another bounty hunter might be rough, or...hell." He ran his hand through his hair.

"A favor? By following me, having pictures of me..." She trailed off.

He didn't know what the hell she was thinking, so he took a guess. "Look, you don't have to go to jail. We'll leave in the morning, get to Santa Barbara in a few hours, and clean this mess up. You'll be fine."

"And you'll get paid for doing me a favor." She turned away from him and dropped the picture on the bed.

Her voice was thin, her bare shoulders tight. There was something else going on here. A dark idea settled in his chest. "That man that you attacked with the staple gun, did he hurt you?"

"No." He watched her back expand as she took a breath. Then she turned, her face grim. "I'll be back in time for the court hearing. Your job is over; you can leave." She walked in a wide arc around him to head for the door.

Her sandals clicked on the tile and sent echoes of unease into the base of his skull. What was he missing? He couldn't let her go. He moved fast, getting to the door before she could open it. "Lexie, stop." He leaned over her, putting his hand on the door. The scent of a flowery lotion, warmed by her body, assaulted him. He had to think. "What are you doing in my room? How did you get in?"

She stared at the door, her fingers around the

handle. "I saw you here and didn't think it was a coincidence. Let me go—"

"My room was locked."

"I'm resourceful."

He nodded to himself, thinking she'd done the same thing he had and gotten a maid to let her in. But why? What made her worried enough to sneak into his room to find out why he was there? "Why didn't you just ask me? I planned to find you and talk to you tonight anyway." He didn't remember her being this paranoid or suspicious.

Her shoulders dropped. "Just cautious. Let me out of the room, Nick."

The fear in her voice cut him. Jesus. "Not until you tell me what the hell you're afraid of. Now."

"Nothing. But I'm not going back yet."

He was done talking to her ponytail. Taking his hand off the door, he reached for her arm.

She jerked, whirling around with her eyes wide. "Let go!"

Startled, he dropped her arm. "What the hell? I'm not going to hurt you. I—"

"Don't touch me." Her voice quavered.

Nick took a breath to calm down. It was clear to him that Lexie was on her last nerve. Scared, maybe even terrified. He'd seen her handle four long days of temper tantrums, wedding-dress disasters, last-minute changes, all the dramas that went with weddings, and she hadn't even broken a sweat.

Right now she looked at him like he might be a monster. What the hell had scared her? He didn't believe for a second she'd had a breakdown, but she was definitely afraid. Stepping to the side, he said quietly, "Go sit down. I won't touch you."

"I'm leaving."

He sighed. "Then I'll touch you. I won't hurt you, but I will stop you from leaving."

She leaned back against the door. "It's not you stalking me, is it?"

Nick blinked. "Stalking you? Like following your trail because I'm a bounty hunter and that's my job, kind of stalking you?"

"Like getting into my apartment, leaving my laptop on, opening my mail, taking underwear..." She clenched her jaw, then added, "Making countless phone calls from different phone numbers and hanging up. Coming into my apartment while I'm in the shower and dumping all my underwear all over my bedroom... I heard someone in my apartment, but by the time I got out of the shower and dressed, they were gone. Just the underwear all over..." She shivered and crossed her arms tightly. "The last straw was finding a note on my car that said, 'Die, bitch.'"

Shit, now her fear made sense. "Jesus," he swore and strode to the bed, then quickly sorted through the paperwork he had on her until he came up with the bond piece. Going back, he handed it to her. "I'm not stalking you. This is what the bond company issues to give me the authority to find you and bring you in."

She took the paper and read it, her mouth thinning in more frustration.

He asked, "If you're being stalked, why haven't you gone to the police?"

Handing the paper back, she leveled her tired gaze on him. "I told them, but it was after the assault charge and they seemed to think I was inventing stories to get the charges dropped. I told them one thing had nothing to do with the other, but they seemed to think I was building some kind of stress defense. Especially since the note on my car was written on my own stationery from my apartment."

"So you saw me here and—" He didn't need to finish. He got the picture. She was scared but no one believed her. Her own lawyer had told Nick she was unstable. To keep from touching her, he moved to the bed to drop the bond piece onto the pile of papers and photos. "Your family?"

"They think I'm trying to get out of work." She pushed off the door and stood up straight. "But I'm handling it. I've hired a PI to watch my apartment while I'm gone. He'll catch the stalker and then I'll go back to Santa Barbara for my court date. You'll get your money. Good night." She turned and reached for the door.

"You should have called me." As soon as he said it, he knew it was stupid. But he was feeling very protective, although he was baffled as to why.

She looked back at him. "For what? A night of sex? And how would I call you, Nick? Look you up under one-night stands in the phone book?"

He winced. Since all he'd ever offered her was sex, and no details about his career, she'd had no reason to think he would or could help her—although as resourceful as she obviously was, she could have gotten his number from his sister. "I deserved that. But I'm here now and I'm going to help you."

Anger narrowed her gaze. She dropped the door handle and turned. "Are you worried I'm going to disappear and you'll be out your bounty hunting fee?"

He crossed his arms over his chest. "Honey, I hate to break it to you, but you're not worth enough money to bother with."

"Then stop bothering!" She turned again, heading back for the door.

Damn, she had to be getting dizzy with the rushing back and forth. He understood her stress, but she needed to trust him—he wasn't the enemy. Nor could he let her walk out. "I'm not going to let you leave my room. If you open that door, I'm going to assume you want my hands on you." He had no idea how she would react.

She halted a foot from the door and turned, her brown gaze meeting his. In a soft voice, she said, "Maybe I do."

Unfolding his arms, he frowned and wondered what the hell she meant. "Do what?"

She shook her head, looking like she'd do anything to take back her words.

She looked beautiful and...raw. Needy. Yet so alone it made him mad, frustrated, and determined. "Don't lie to me now." He advanced on her, and he was going to be ticked if she dared to be afraid of him. He'd understood it when she didn't know why he was there, but now she did know.

She leaned back slightly. "I guess I haven't forgotten that kiss."

He smiled then. "Good to know I'm not the only one."

"But you weren't interested after you kissed me."

That surprised the hell out of him. "What gave you that idea?"

"You told me to go home."

Women. Christ. "You told me no. One kiss and you were reconsidering—we both know you would have regretted that."

She curved her lips into a teasing smirk. "Ha. I scared you."

That made him grin. "Yeah. I think you did. You're not an easy woman to walk away from."

She shrugged. "Okay, bounty hunter, what now? If you won't let me leave, and I won't go back to Santa Barbara with you, we seem to be at a standoff."

He put his hand on the door over her head and leaned close to her face. "You're in my custody now. That'll get the lawyers and bail bondsmen to shut up for a few days. Together we'll figure out how to deal with your stalker."

Lexie's fingers tapped out a steady rhythm on the keyboard of her laptop. The night was quiet, and through the closed door she could hear the waves crashing against the shore. She considered opening the sliding glass door to let in the sea breeze, but that didn't seem wise at 1:00 a.m.

Every sentence she typed increased her sense of accomplishment. She was heading into the home stretch of her book. Her heroine's life hung in the balance, as did those of the hostages. Even she was on edge, and she knew the heroine would live.

Unfortunately one or two of the hostages wouldn't be as fortunate, but...

A squeak and click startled the bejeebers out of her. Jerking her head up from staring at the screen, she tried to place the noise. Her heart banged against her chest wall. What was that?

She didn't hear anything else. She wasn't even sure what direction the noise came from. The door to the room was on the left of where she sat on the bed, propped up by pillows. The sliding glass door covered with blackout drapes was on her right. The room was large, with the walls done in a hand-troweled texture of green and white. There was mosaic tile on the floor, with colorful rugs. The tile could make the room echo, especially in the quiet of the night.

Her heart rate calmed down.

With her attention diverted from her book, her mind wandered to Nick.

Nick Vardolous. Here. At Sand Castle Resort. And he was hotter than she remembered. Those eyes...oh hell, all of him. He'd been her fantasy man since that kiss. A safe man to fantasize about, but she hadn't expected to meet up with him again.

It rankled that she was nothing more than a job

to him. Which she knew was ridiculous. They hadn't had a relationship; they hadn't even had sex.

At least he had believed her when she told him about her stalker. Then he'd checked out her private investigator, Tate Zuckerman, and told her she'd made an excellent choice. He treated her like an intelligent woman, although he had insisted on checking out her room for any danger, then confiscated her car keys before he agreed to leave her in her room.

Nick. He did something to her, made her feel safe and sexy. That kind of charm should be...

A tapping noise scared the hell out of her. She shoved her laptop off her legs and leaped off the bed.

What was it? It came from the patio sliding glass door. Was someone out there?

Her heart pounded in her ears, her blood rushing so fast she was dizzy. Standing on the cold tile floor, she sucked in a breath. *Think.*

Thunk, thunk, thunk.

Oh God! Someone was out there! Nine-one-one was the first thing she thought.

Then Nick. He was closer. She grabbed the phone and dialed his room number.

He answered on the first ring. "Vardolous."

"Nick! It's Lexie. Someone is pounding on my sliding glass door. I don't..."

"On my way." He hung up.

The sliding glass door rattled. Someone was trying to open it, but it was locked. Then a voice called out, "I know you're awake! I see the light on!"

She didn't recognize the voice. She shivered, wrapping her arms around herself and backing up until she felt the solid wall behind her. Was it her stalker? Maybe a random killer?

He yelled again, "I just want to talk to—oomph!"

Lexie blinked and leaned forward. All she could hear was shuffling and a thump. Nick?

Her phone rang. The shrill sound arrowed right through her. Grabbing it, she said, "What?"

Nick answered, "Lexie, it's me. I have the guy. He has press credentials."

"A reporter?" Her voice climbed as the adrenaline spiked in her bloodstream.

"Drunk reporter." Nick's voice was knife edged with disgust. "Security is taking him away."

"Oh. Okay. Thank you, I—"

"Open your door."

"My door?"

"I'm right outside your door. Not the slider, the door. Check the peephole, then open it."

She did as he instructed and sure enough, Nick stood outside her door with his cell phone to his ear. She hung up the phone, undid the locks, and opened it.

He closed his phone, walked in, and shut the door behind him.

Lexie backed up and stared. Nick took up a lot of room. He was half naked, only wearing a pair of loose-fit jeans hanging low on his hips. His black hair was tousled and his jaw shadowed with a dark beard that set off his green bedroom eyes. In the glow of her bedside lamp, his gold-toned skin stretched over some serious muscle in his shoulders and chest. He looked hot and tasty. It had to be some kind of adrenaline high channeling her thoughts to naked skin and sizzling sex. She forced herself to get under control.

"You okay?" His voice was low and tight.

No. She wasn't okay. Stalkers, getting arrested, a ticked-off family, drunk reporters, and a way-too-sexy bounty hunter were ripping away control over her own life. She was tired, scared, lonely, and stunned that Nick came to her rescue. She couldn't remember anyone ever doing that for her. It was always Lexie who fixed things.

"Lexie?"

She pulled herself together. "Sure. I'm fine. I'm always fine. It's a family rule…" Jeez, that made no freaking sense. Closing her eyes, she leaned back against the wall and brought her hand up to rub her eyes. "Sorry, I'm a little rattled, but fine. Thank you for dealing with this for me. I realize now I could have just called security myself. Sorry I bothered you."

"Now you're pissing me off."

No big surprise there. She dropped her hand and opened her eyes. "You're going to have to get in line."

Nick drew his eyebrows together in a thunderous expression. "Say what?"

"There's a line of people mad at me." Why didn't she just shut up? And why did Nick have to look so hot? She dropped her gaze to his seriously ripped chest. He had sinewy muscles, not the gym kind, but the lean muscle of an active man. The deep urge to lean on some of that muscle was an unexpected weakness. A new weakness, that's great, just what she needed—a bad case of Man Hungry on top of everything else. It'd been almost a year since she'd felt a man wrap his body around hers, slide inside her, make her feel valuable and real. The silence stretched out.

"Look at me."

His command captured her full attention.

His darkly stubbled jaw emphasized the liquid gold floating in his light green eyes. "While we're here, if you're in trouble, you're going to call me first."

Just nod, she told herself, desperate and tired of being alone. She knew she was too vulnerable, feeling too impulsive to trust her mouth. Opening her mouth to agree, she blurted out, "Even for sex?"

Chapter 3

NICK TOOK A STEP TOWARD her before his brain kicked in. It was the damned pink panties. When she'd opened the door and he'd seen her wearing a thin pink tank top, she'd taken his breath away.

Then he'd seen the panties and his blood went south. He'd hardened so fast it was a wonder he didn't get dizzy.

Clenching his fists, he knew his hard-on strained against his pants. "Lexie—"

She stepped up to him and put her hand on his chest. "I'm tired of being cautious and worrying about tomorrow. I want to try impulsive."

He caught her hand and inhaled. Damn, she smelled like that flower, night jasmine or whatever, mixed with warm skin. His whole body throbbed with hard-core lust. They were both on adrenaline overload. He could control this, he would control it. "No. No sex." He barely got the words out.

Her body deflated, and her hand slid from his grasp. "Okay. Thanks again, Nick. I'll call you if I'm in trouble, but not for sex. Good night." She reached for the door.

She was making him crazy, infuriating him. He wanted her naked and under him, looking up with unfocused eyes while he drove himself into her. He wanted her breath to hitch and pant as she lost control, her body shivering and spasming with pleasure while he watched.

Then she had the nerve to pull open her door, put a hand on her hip, and stare at him expectantly.

He had to shock them both back to reality. "If anyone walks by, they are going to see you in your panties."

She looked down. The expression on her face was priceless—total shock.

Nick reached over, closed the door, and locked it. Then he turned to see Lexie walking quickly to her dresser. Away from him. Her tight ass covered by the sheer pink panties twitching in her rush. He was going to burst into flames. Before he realized it, he was moving. He scooped her up in his arms.

"Nick! What are you doing!"

"Putting you in your bed and covering you up before I do something stupid." He all but dropped her on the bed and wrenched the covers up over her.

She sat up, leaning back against the pillows. "I'm not going to attack you!"

He stared down at her.

Her gaze moved to his crotch. Then her gaze slid up. "Oh."

"I don't get emotionally or sexually involved with

my work. Ever." He'd learned that the hard way, and he never forgot the lesson.

She blinked, her mouth tightening as she seemed to battle with herself, then she lowered her gaze back to his crotch. She jerked her head, looking everywhere but at him. "Okay. Got it. You should leave now."

Nick leaned down, putting a hand on either side of her hips so he was nose to nose with her. "I'm not leaving you alone so another lunatic can break in here. I'm staying. And if you don't stop talking, or wiggling that prime ass of yours in front of me, I'm going to strip you down to your skin and fuck you until you're screaming my name in pleasure, over and over. And then when I regain my senses and realize that I screwed up, I will be forced to take you back to Santa Barbara immediately and insist that you be locked up in a cell where you're safe until we find your stalker. Your choice."

"I'll stop talking."

The phone woke her up. "Hello?"

"It's nine in the morning! And you're sleeping!"

At the sound of her brother's irritated voice, Lexie snapped awake. "Larry? How'd you find me?" She sat up in bed and looked around. The patio lounge chair had a pillow and rumpled blanket on it...

The night came back to her, the memory of Nick sleeping in her room. Where was he?

"By calling all the hotels in your honeymoon file.

What the hell is the matter with you, Lexie? How can you be so selfish? Mom's having chest pains. She had to do two weddings and you know she's not up to it after her heart attack! Amber is hysterical. Dad is threatening to cut you out of the will. Clients are screaming. You have to get your ass back to work!"

She shoved her heavy hair out of her face, heard the shower turn off, and assumed Nick was in there. Throwing her legs over the side of the bed, she forced herself to deal with her brother. "Mom is fine. The doctor said she could go back to work months ago." Her sister, Amber, had been hysterical from the day she was born; that was nothing new.

"You were always selfish, Lexie, but I never thought you'd pull something like this. One of the cakes for a wedding this weekend was wrong. *Wrong!* The Pattersons screamed at me for a whole hour. I don't have time to fix your screw-ups. I'm running a business, and you know Patricia and I are buying a house and selling our condo. How could you just run away and leave us all to clean up your mess?"

She knew damn well it wasn't her screwup, but Larry's. Her brother was lazy and she had to double-check every cake order he did, just as her mom had done. Fatigue weighed down her shoulders as she dropped her gaze to the green mosaic pattern in the white tile. "I didn't run away..."

"Yes, you did. You left us all in a bind. Mom is

afraid to book any weddings. She's afraid! She had a heart attack, remember? And just how am I going to make a living, huh, Lexie? We have a potential buyer for the condo, which means I have to worry about a bigger mortgage on the new house. Does it always have to be about you?"

Shame pressed down on her chest. She really thought her mom had been taking advantage of her. That she'd had her first taste of real freedom after being a workaholic for decades. But maybe she was wrong, maybe the heart attack had damaged her mom's confidence. "Is Mom all right?"

"No! What have I been telling you! And I need more cake orders. You have to come back."

Her stomach cramped with real fear. "I can't, not yet. Larry, someone has been getting into my apartment. If you know anything..."

He cut her off with a rude noise. "Don't start that shit again. You're ruining my life, trying to blame me because you can't remember using your laptop or keep track of your clothes. I was in your apartment once, once! It was a mistake. I'm under a lot of pressure here, Lexie."

Right, and screwing a woman who wasn't his wife in Lexie's apartment was the obvious way of relieving pressure. She wouldn't have found out if her dumb brother hadn't left the condom wrapper on her nightstand. It hadn't taken Lexie long to figure out he'd swiped her house key from their mom. "I'm not trying to ruin you. I just need to figure out who is getting into..."

"For God's sake, stop thinking about yourself.

We're all sick of it. Especially Harry. He doesn't even come around anymore. He's too humiliated after you attacked him and caused his fiancée to dump him right before the wedding."

A noise made her look up.

Nick stood there. His hair was shower wet, his skin still damp, and his expression was ice cold. "Who are you talking to?"

She put her hand over the mouthpiece. "My brother."

He reached over and took the phone from her. "Your sister is being threatened by a stalker. Any idea who it might be?"

Lexie was stunned. No one took control from her like that. She stood up to grab the phone back.

Nick slung his arm around her shoulders and held her to his side.

She heard her brother bellowing that Lexie was just trying to get out of work when her family needed her, and something about her making wild accusations. It was easier to concentrate on the feel of Nick's chest expanding as he breathed, along with his warm, damp skin scented with the soap from his shower. She sank into the pleasure of having his arm around her and wondered when she had become this pathetic.

"Now I know why she ran." He leaned over and slammed the phone down.

Lexie took the opportunity to put some distance between them. It was one thing to think about seducing Nick in the middle of the night. Before he knew that she'd run out on her family. That her own family didn't believe her. Shame and embarrassment rolled around her gut. But she faced Nick. Better to just get it over with.

He turned on her. "You're not going back there until it's safe. You sure as hell can't count on your asshole brother to help you."

She bristled. Only she could call her brother an asshole. "Don't talk about my brother like that. It's a lot of work to own a bakery, plus he's selling his condo and he's worried about our mom. He depends on wedding cake orders from My Perfect Wedding."

He stepped toward her. "Then he's a leech and an asshole. Let him get his own damned cake orders. If you were my sister, I'd have looked into this stalker situation the first time you told me."

He was close enough to kiss her. And it hit her that she only had on her sleep shirt and panties. She felt her face heat at the memory of his reaction to her panties last night. She needed distance, now. She couldn't risk him dragging her back to Santa Barbara. "Your sister is lucky. I'm going to take a shower. There's no reason for you to stay here, I'm perfectly safe." She escaped into the bathroom and closed the door.

Once she finished showering, she decided on her black bikini. She'd brought two with her and kept them in the bathroom to dry out. Brushing out her wet hair, she looked into the fogged mirror. She decided against blow-drying and left her hair down. Opening the door, she walked into the cool room.

"You're trying to kill me."

She jumped, her heart slamming in her chest. And yet, part of her was pleased. Nick sat at the table by the sliding glass door, drinking a cup of coffee from the in-room coffeemaker and reading the complimentary newspaper.

"I thought you'd left."

He ran his gaze down her length and back up to her face. "I should have and saved myself. Jesus, Lexie."

Was that a compliment or insult? And since he'd made his position on sex with her clear, why did she care? "It's just a bathing suit." She went to the closet, pulled out the wraparound dress she used as a cover-up, and shoved her arms in it. Concentrating on tying the strings to secure the dress, she added, "No one's stopping you from leaving now."

Nick stood up and approached her. "I'm not an asshole like your brother. That's what is stopping me."

He was close behind her, too close. Shoving her feet into her flip-flops, she said, "Stop calling my brother that."

"Stop defending him."

She turned to him. The room was flooded with daylight, and Nick looked even more gorgeous. His hair was dry, black as night, and had a slight wave. His eyes focused on her. There was no more hiding. "My mom had a heart attack. I took over running My Perfect Wedding for her. For a year, I hated every single minute of it. I begged my mom to come back, but she kept putting me off. Then the groom,

34

William Harry Livingston, got drunk at the rehearsal dinner and flashed me. I lost it and stapled his pants to his waist. Then the arrest, the stories in the tabloids, my stalker... I just left. I went to my parents' house, dumped all the open files for upcoming weddings on my mom's table, told her it was her business, not mine, and left." She stopped talking. What else was there to say?

"Back up. Livingston exposed himself and that's why you stapled him?"

She studied his chest. "Yes."

"Then why the hell were you arrested?"

Startled, she backed up a step. "Because I didn't report it. I figured he was just drunk and stressed. I was arrested the next day when he filed a complaint against me. I told everyone..." She took a breath. "This isn't getting us anywhere. The point is that my brother—"

"Is an asshole."

"Will you stop—"

He reached out and tugged her to him, close enough that she could see the icy anger in his eyes. "Did I miss the part where your brother found Livingston and beat the shit out of him? How about your dad? Did anyone in your family take your side? Back you up?" His eyes bored into her.

"It's not like that—"

"No? It sounds like they blame you and side with Livingston."

Embarrassed, she wasn't going to tell him that Larry took Harry's side because Harry brought him business from his real estate connections. Instead, she blurted out, "I can take care of myself. I could have handled Harry better, he was just drunk and stupid." A pocket of air caught in her chest. In order for her family to love her, she had to be the good girl. Part of her had thought when she dropped everything and left, they'd realize she was in trouble. That she needed them for a change. It didn't happen.

He let her go.

She glared at him, desperate to get away. "You have my car keys, Nick, I'm not going anywhere. All I'm going to do is get something to eat, go to the beach, and work on my laptop. Alone."

He opened his mouth.

She was at the edge of her endurance. "Please, just leave me alone."

Nick drank his beer and stretched out his legs. People were milling around the balcony bar overlooking the ocean. The cool breeze did nothing to calm his lust.

Damn Lexie and that bikini. He'd managed to keep tabs on her all day, and she'd done just as she said she would. She'd spent time sitting on the beach working on her laptop. After lunch, she'd stowed her laptop and swum in the pool. Then she'd disappeared into her room, probably to sleep.

Nick had talked to her PI, Tate Zuckerman. Tate was an ex-cop, and it turned out that he and Nick had some mutual friends with the Santa Barbara

Sheriff's Department. Those friends had vouched for Tate and evidently told Tate that Nick was an okay guy. Lexie had given the PI permission to tell him anything related to her stalker, but unfortunately, Tate had nothing, not a single sign of her stalker hanging around the apartment. The PI was worried and said he was going to talk to people in Lexie's life to see if something popped. Nick swore under his breath. Her stalker should be agitated by now, hanging around, looking for any sign of Lexie.

It was Monday. They had four more days until Lexie had to be back for court at 9:00 a.m. on Friday.

He couldn't take one more day of watching her and wanting her. She was getting under his skin, threatening his self-control. He couldn't help but admire her resiliency in spite of her family's lack of support. She had found a very good PI and hired him, then removed herself from the situation. Smart, resourceful, and so damned sexy his dick wasn't listening to his brain.

But he couldn't take her back to Santa Barbara if they didn't know who or where her stalker was.

A man dropped into the chair next to him, jarring him out of his thoughts.

"Rough night, Vardolous?"

Nick nodded to Mac Koontz, head of security at Sand Castle Resort. They went way back. Koontz wore slacks and a blue and white polo shirt with a Sand Castle logo on the pocket. "Lounge-chair sleeping sucks."

Koontz laughed. "Your questionable charm didn't get you into her bed, huh?"

He turned his gaze to Koontz. "I don't mix sex and work."

Mac's face tightened. "I thought you were putting it behind you. It's been eight years. Let Ellen go."

Nick stared at him. "I watched her die, I let her go. But I haven't forgotten that I screwed up and got her killed."

Mac stared back with his intense blue eyes. "The fact is that no amount of martial arts will win against a gun." He took a deep breath. "We both learned that. You walked away, Nick, but you never stopped training or teaching. You're making the right decision getting back in now. All you have to do is sign those papers and we're partners once again."

He forced his clenched hands to relax. "You're awfully sure I'll sign the partnership papers." He loved karate, and through those long, dark days after Ellen's death, karate kept him sane. He taught some classes at a friend's studio. He had done what he could as a bounty hunter to put the past behind him. More and more, he wanted to get back into teaching karate full time in his own place.

Sighing, Mac said, "We sold our studio because neither one of us could deal with what had happened. But we're older now, and it's time to get back to it." Looking at Nick, he added, "Share a little of our life experience. Give students a foundation for the shit life throws at them, you know?"

He knew. And it was too close to the truth for Nick, so he grinned. "Marriage is making you old and soft."

Mac raised his eyebrows. "Maybe, but I'm getting it every night too."

Nick let the dark memories slide away. "You're damned lucky. Shelly's too good for you."

"I'm off duty now. Come over, we'll barbecue, make margaritas."

He shook his head. "Can't. Got a skip in my custody." Cozy domestic scenes weren't his thing.

"Bring her. Lexie is a nice woman. I've gotten to know her a little bit while she's been here, and everyone loves her. She's friendly to all the staff, making her an instant favorite guest. She can't really be a fugitive." Mac shook his head.

"It's a bogus charge." Nick stared at the cold bottle. Lexie was doing something to him. To his guts. She was reaching into him and finding the man he'd once wanted to be.

Before he'd let his emotions make a decision that caused a woman he loved to suffer a brutal death.

That man was gone, dead, and it ticked him off that Lexie made him remember. Made him want to be the kind of man worthy of a woman like her.

Of her.

And the worst part now, nobody stood up for Lexie. She'd been doing it all herself, and when her world crumbled, her asshole brother yelled at her.

He realized Koontz was talking and tore his gaze from the bottle. "What?"

Dark eyes locked in on him. "Oh shit, Vardolous. You're falling for her."

"No. I'm doing my job." As a courtesy to his old friend, Nick had gone to see Koontz first thing, declared why he was at the resort and that the apprehension would be low key. Mac had been surprised by the idea of Lexie being a fugitive. "There's a complication. Lexie has had some trouble with a stalker back in Santa Barbara. We're hoping a PI she hired can catch him before I take her back."

Mac studied him. "Think he'll track her?"

Who knew with these freaks? "She was easy to find."

He nodded. "I'll tell the staff to be on the lookout."

"Thanks." Wouldn't hurt to have another layer of protection.

Mac regarded him thoughtfully. "I can help with security. Can't do anything about your feelings for Lexie."

Nick kept himself under tight control. She was in trouble, and he had to stay clearheaded to help her while doing his job. Sex and intimacy clouded judgment. "I don't have feelings for her. She's a job, nothing more. The sooner I get Lexie Rollins off my hands, the better."

Mac lifted his gaze behind Nick and winced.

The hair on the back of Nick's neck stood up. "Shit." He turned around to see Lexie standing there. She had on a pretty sundress, her hair flowing in soft waves in a sharp contrast to her tight mouth and wide eyes. Before he could react, she turned around to walk away. Jumping up, Nick said, "Lexie, I just meant that—"

She turned and the skirt of her sundress whirled around her legs. Color rushed into her cheeks while her eyes shimmered with either anger or unshed tears. "I know what you meant. I'm going to get some dinner. I came to let you know in case you were hungry, but now I think eating together is a bad idea." She walked away.

Mac hurried past him. "Lexie, hey!" He caught her arm. Nick watched her shoulders tighten, then relax when she saw it was Mac.

"Lexie, come have dinner with my wife and me. We have plenty of food. Shelly was hoping Nick would come over, but he turned me down. Besides, she'll like you much better than she likes Nick."

Furious, Nick closed the space between them. "She's not going anywhere."

Lexie ignored him. "Would you mind giving me a ride? Nick confiscated my car keys. I can grab a taxi to come back."

Like hell she would. "I'll drive you. I'm not letting you leave the resort without me."

She frowned at Mac. "I thought Nick wasn't going? I've changed my mind, I'll stay here and eat."

It was slowly sinking into his head that Lexie had dressed up a little bit. She put on makeup, brushed out her long hair, and wore high-heeled sandals. She'd come looking for him, planning to ask him to have dinner. Then he'd gone and hurt her feelings. Damn it. He walked over and shoulder-bumped Mac out of his way. "Lexie, I just meant that I will feel better when you're safe."

"You'll feel better when you get your money." She barely spared a glance for him. "Thanks for the invitation, Mac. Maybe another time when I'm free of my current situation."

Him? Was she talking about *him*?

Mac didn't give him a chance to ask. "Lexie, please reconsider. Shelly would love to meet you. Nick can come if he wants to, but I'll make sure he doesn't bother you."

Now he *bothered* her? Frowning, Nick crossed his arms over his chest. "I go where she goes."

Both of them ignored him. Lexie said, "Are you sure your wife won't mind?"

Mac's face split in a grin. "No. I'll bring you back tonight and make sure you get in your room safely."

Damn it, when did he disappear? "I'll bring her back."

"Thanks, Mac." Lexie walked off with him toward the employee parking lot.

Nick stood there by himself. "What the hell just happened?"

Chapter 4

"ANOTHER MARGARITA?"

Lexie grinned up at Mac as he poured the chilled drink into her glass. "I'm not driving, why not?" Two margaritas and she felt no pain.

Well, less pain, anyway.

Nick's comment about getting her off his hands had hurt. She had put on a dress, done her makeup and thought maybe they could go to dinner and at least be friends.

She'd been wrong. He couldn't wait to get rid of her and pick up his money.

Sipping her margarita, she felt Nick's gaze on her from where he sat on her left. They were in Mac and Shelly's lush backyard, eating crab legs. Three of them were having a good time.

Nick appeared to be brooding. He'd been in a gloomy mood since he'd shown up at the house one minute after Mac and Lexie had arrived in Mac's car. At least she hadn't had to ride with Nick and feel his urgency to get rid of her.

From across the table, Shelly said, "So tell us about yourself, Lexie. How did you manage to get Super Bounty Hunter on your trail?"

"Ha. Funny." Nick picked up his iced tea and drank it.

Lexie considered suggesting that one or two margaritas might restore his sense of humor, but she decided to ignore him. She was having fun in spite of him. Shelly was one of those beautiful women you couldn't hate because she was nice with a quirky sense of humor. Mac had a tendency to touch her every few minutes in the unconscious way of lovers. As much as Lexie hated the wedding planning business, she had seen real love occasionally, and these two had it.

Shelly shot Nick a frown, then said to Lexie, "I shouldn't have asked, maybe you don't want to tell us."

Shrugging, Lexie explained about William Harry Livingston and the staple gun.

Shelly burst out laughing while Mac looked bemused. He said, "You can't be serious. They're charging you with assault and battery for that?" He looked over at Nick. "I'm thinking we need to pay this guy a visit."

"Hell, yeah. But it'll have to wait until this stalker problem is resolved."

Lexie swiveled her gaze between Mac and Nick. Then she looked at Shelly. "What are they talking about?"

"Defending your honor or whatever the

enlightened Neanderthals are calling it this year."
Shelly shrugged and picked up her drink.

"That's ridiculous." Even though she was on her
third drink and a little looped, Lexie still couldn't
believe Nick and Mac were serious. Mac hardly
knew her, and Nick couldn't wait to get rid of her.

Shelly set her glass down. "They don't get that
women can take care of themselves. Just ignore
them."

Nick snorted. "Ask Lexie what her asshole
brother did about the groom exposing himself, then
filing charges against her."

"Nick!" She turned to glare at him. "Don't call
my brother that. I told you..."

He stared right back at her. "That he leeches off
your mom, and now you. I remember. Any other
leeching siblings?"

"Amber is not a leech! She's young, and she's
just getting her photography business going. You
don't know anything about my family."

"They all use you and leech off you. Don't want
to know any more than that."

Loneliness wrapped around her, making her
suddenly feel separated from the three of them. For
a couple hours, she'd been part of the group. Until
Nick opened his big mouth and told Mac and Shelly
that her own family didn't support her. Anger roiled
inside her, fueled by the margaritas. "What makes
you so different from them? I'm no more than a
bounty to you." Crap, too late she realized she was
practically yelling. She looked at Shelly and Mac,
who'd been so nice to her. "Sorry."

Nick grabbed her shoulders, forcing her to look at him. "The difference is that I believe you. I won't let anyone hurt you. If anyone tries, I'll hurt them. Does that clear it up for you?"

Stunned stupid, she sat there like a lump. Why? Why would he do that? Until she finally remembered. "Because I'm your job?"

He let go of her, turned back to look into his glass. "Yes."

Shelly blew out a long breath. "Nick, you're an idiot. I've never seen you act like this."

Lexie took control. "It's okay, Shelly. He's being honest. It's not a big deal." It was to her, but she could keep that to herself. She drained her margarita.

Shelly smiled encouragingly. "So you don't like wedding planning. What do you want to do?"

Looking up into Shelly's pretty dark eyes, Lexie surprised herself by saying, "I want to write. Um, books. Thrillers."

Shelly perked up. "Really? I love to read! Are you writing something now?"

Lexie told herself not to think about Nick sitting beside her and judging her. "I was in the UCLA writing program but when my mom had her heart attack I dropped out to take over My Perfect Wedding."

Nick snorted. "Right."

That did it. Hadn't she heard it all her life? That she wasn't ever going to make it as a writer, so she needed to be realistic and take over My Perfect Wedding? That her dream was selfish and stupid?

That she was the plain ordinary sibling, not the creative type like Larry and Amber? Tears burned at the back of her eyes and clogged her throat, but she wouldn't let Nick Vardolous make her cry. She wouldn't let anyone make her cry. Anger was easier. "I don't care what you or my family think. I *am* writing my book. I'm almost done. And I'm not doing it to prove anything to you or them. I'm doing it for me." She stood up and realized her head was a little fuzzy from the drinks. Carefully she turned her back on Nick and asked Mac and Shelly, "May I use your phone to call a cab?"

Mac met her gaze. "I'll take you back, Lexie."

Nick said, "I'll take her."

She shook her head, then got dizzy and had to grab the edge of the table. It was hard to hold on to her dignity and the table while everyone stared at her, but she did her best. "I'll just get a cab. Thank you for dinner." She escaped inside the house before anyone could stop her. Finding a phone in the kitchen, she picked it up to dial information.

Nick came in. "Put the phone down."

Lexie shook her head. She leaned over to the kitchen window to look out and saw that Mac and Shelly were still sitting outside.

Nick took the phone from her hand and set it down. He trapped her between his body and the counter. "Shelly's right. You're turning me into an idiot. I can't think around you."

Frowning, she wondered just how drunk she was.

He moved his hands up her bare arms. "I believe

you, Lexie. You can tell me anything and I believe you."

She wanted to look away, but his gaze held her captive. "You didn't. Not about my book."

He threaded his fingers into her hair. "I did. And I believe you left school to rescue your family. It just pisses me off that you did. They don't deserve you. And you deserve much better than them."

Why was he being nice to her? He stood so close that she could smell the scent of his soap mixed with his body heat. He made her feel small and protected, and it confused her. "I must be drunk. I never drink more than one drink." She closed her eyes to escape his stare. "I just want to be impulsive and free for once."

"You're not drunk. You were feeling loose and happy until I ruined it for you." He lowered his head. "I can't do this." He said the words and pressed his mouth to hers.

She was drunk, she had to be, because she put her arms around him. Nick slid one hand to her bare upper back, pressing her closer to him. Then he said against her lips, "More, Lexie."

She opened her mouth, feeling the slide of his tongue fill her. Heat washed over her, and raw need filled the gaping loneliness inside her. Running her hands over him, she explored the hard ridge of muscles. Everything else drained from her thoughts but Nick.

Until he made a noise and lifted his head. His green eyes were almost all gold. "We can't. I can't risk it."

Cold dread mixed with embarrassment. "Right. I'm your job."

He wrapped his hand around a length of her hair, gently tilting her head back. "Because you matter. I won't screw up and let you get hurt or dead just because I'm horny. I did that once, and Ellen died." He dragged in a breath. "She was murdered right in front of me."

Nick had the TV on and tried desperately not to think of Lexie in the bed a few feet away. She had her laptop opened, he presumed to work on her book, but the typing had stalled. She had to be tired. Propped up on the uncomfortable lounge chair wearing only his pants, he flipped channels and hoped something would catch his attention.

"You live here, in San Diego, don't you? You knew exactly where Mac and Shelly lived. You and Mac seem to have a history together, like you've been friends a long time."

He could practically hear her thinking. "Yes." Before he could stop himself, he added, "I'm not home much." But that was going to change.

"Ellen's murder happened here, in San Diego?"

He stared hard at the TV. "I'm not going to talk about it."

"I'll give you the bed if you'll tell me."

"Go to sleep, Lexie."

In his peripheral vision, he saw her set the laptop aside and scoot to the end of the bed. "You can't sleep in that chair, you're too big. I'll trade you even if you won't tell me."

She was probably tormenting him on purpose. She had on panties, a tank top, and way too much skin showing. Gritting his teeth, he said, "Get back in that bed."

"Tell me about Ellen."

He looked over at her. Her eyes were heavy from the alcohol and fatigue. She sat cross-legged. Dropping his eyes, he saw her nipples pebbled against the thin shirt, her slightly rounded belly, her thighs spread, and...the powder blue panties barely covering her.

His dick snapped to attention. He threw his arm over his eyes. "You're making me pay for hurting your feelings."

"I...uh...no. I just thought you'd feel better if you talked about Ellen."

He lifted his arm off his face and looked at her sincere stare. "Why?"

She met his gaze. "Because I saw the pain in your eyes when you told me tonight. I don't want you to hurt so much, Nick."

Shit. "Trying to fix me, Lexie? With your family out of reach, am I your project?"

He heard the movement on the bed. Maybe she'd leave him the hell alone. Then her warm hand touched his chest.

His balls seized up with raw lust.

She said, "Go take the bed. I'll leave you alone."

He grabbed her hand and pulled her down on top of him. To his surprise, she went boneless, letting him catch her weight. The contact warmed him and inflamed his lust. "You're so stubborn." He put his hand over her head, cradling her face to his chest. He just wanted to hold her. Was that so wrong?

Softly, she said, "Be glad I don't have my staple gun."

He laughed. Damn, she was funny. His cock throbbed, but having her on top of him, feeling her take each breath, eased the old pain in him.

She moved her hand, laying her spread fingers and palm on his chest. "Nick, how long ago did she die?"

"Eight years." Hell, she'd slipped that answer out of him by distracting him.

"What happened?"

"If I tell you, will you promise to go to sleep?"

She took a breath, expanding her breasts against him. "I'll promise to shut up. Best offer."

He stroked her hair, enjoying the soft feel of it. "Eight years ago I owned a karate studio with Mac." He felt her start to talk and said, "Let me tell it all or I won't do it."

She nodded.

"I had a student, Ellen. She was learning straight self-defense. I moved her to Mac's class and started dating her. Eventually I learned that her ex-husband had been arrested for drugs and got out on bond. Ellen was going to testify against him. He was calling her, threatening her, and she was scared. I was convinced that Mac and I could protect her. After all, we were both black belts, young, and we thought we were invincible." He stopped talking, the memories bitter.

She lay quietly on top of him. Just her hand moved, stroking his chest in gentle circles.

Nick ran his hand down the length of her hair, and farther to the small of her back. She felt warm and solid and made the memory bearable. He went on. "We hadn't made love because her ex had been a brute. We were going slow. One night at her place, we both got hot and horny. I never gave her safety a thought. I just got us both naked and was deep inside her when her ex-husband broke in." His body involuntarily tightened at the memory.

Lexie kept stroking his chest, the feel of her hands soothing the old agony deep inside him. His muscles relaxed. But she didn't say anything. Not a word.

He took a breath and forced the words out. "I jumped off her, sure I could handle anything. He had a gun and shot Ellen before I could get to him. I still remember her ragged scream of pain as I slammed into him. I knocked him unconscious. I would have killed him." His whole body tightened and strained against the vivid memory. "But Ellen was bleeding. I had to try to stop it."

Lexie lifted her head, and gazed into his eyes.

He was stunned to see her eyes were bright with unshed tears. "She was dead by the time the paramedics got there."

"Nick—"

The memory gnawed at him, but worse was the fear that it could happen to Lexie. She was so vital, so alive, and she deserved a good life. He shifted her off him, and when she stood up, he looked into her face and told her the brutal truth. "Now you know the reason I keep my emotions in check, and I don't mix sex and work."

Chapter 5

NICK WOKE UP TO AN empty room. Leaping off the lounge chair, he checked the bathroom.

No Lexie.

Where the hell did she go? His heart pounding, he grabbed the phone and dialed Mac's cell phone.

"Koontz."

"Lexie's not in the room. I woke up and she's gone." How the hell did she get out without him hearing her? But he knew. Lexie had fallen asleep with her computer on. Nick had gotten up, moved the computer, and damned if he didn't start reading.

He'd read for hours.

Lexie could write. It'd been 2:00 a.m. when he finally fell into a dead sleep.

"She's with Shelly."

"Where?" he demanded, a sick feeling he couldn't quite identify washing over him.

"Surfing. Shelly and Lexie had breakfast and decided to sign up for the surfing lessons. Perfectly safe."

His heart rate slowed. Nick sank down on the bed. "She could have left a note or something." Christ, he sounded like her mother.

Mac snorted. "She wants to have fun, be impulsive before she has to go back and face the charges against her. Not worry about being *your job.*" He hung up.

Nick slammed the phone down. Before he could stop it, he remembered the feel of Lexie stretched out on top of him. How she'd coaxed him into telling her about Ellen. For those few moments, Lexie had been his. He'd shared more of himself with her than he had any woman. That was all the more reason to keep his distance from her—just as soon as he made sure for himself that she was safe.

He hauled ass to his room, grabbed a shower, yanked on his board shorts, and hit the beach. To do a visual check. Lexie was in his custody, and he had to keep tabs on her.

Walking over the cool, slightly damp sand, he caught a few women watching him. Once he freed himself of Lexie, maybe he should come back and check out the scenery. Hole up for a day or two with a nice, willing woman.

Maybe he was just horny.

Once he finished this job, he'd go back to his hit-and-run sex—that would cure his Lexie-lust. Sex with no emotions, and keep it separate from work. It had worked for him for years, and no one got hurt. He wasn't going to let Lexie screw it up.

Where the hell was she? He scanned the sand but didn't see her, although the cabanas blocked much of his view. Mac had said she was surfing, so she was probably with a group. Shielding his eyes, he looked out to the waves. A group of about five women straddled surfboards while two men helped them.

Nick spotted Lexie. She was in a red bikini, and a man had his hand on her lower back, explaining something.

Anger surged inside him. Was she out of her mind? She didn't know that man. He could be dangerous. Without thinking, Nick stormed out into the water.

A wave came up behind the women. They all lay flat on their boards, pushing up on their palms to position themselves to try and catch the wave.

Nick's gut tightened. He surfed all the time and he knew the dangers. Lexie was a novice! She could get hurt. Helplessly, he stood in knee-high water and watched as the wave caught beneath her board. She got her feet under her and stood, balancing on the board.

Her face lit up in joy. Even from a distance, he could see her huge smile right up until she lost her balance and fell off the board.

Nick swam toward her, grabbing her arm and jerking her toward him. She sputtered. "What...oh. Nick. Did you see me? I was surfing! I did it! I got up!"

Her tiny top barely contained her breasts as she panted with excitement. Looking down into her face, he said, "Yes. And I saw that man with his hands all over you too. Is that what you left the room for? To go find some guy to feel you up?" What the fuck was he saying? He was out of his mind.

The happiness in her eyes dimmed. "Let go of me."

"Nick? What are you doing here?" Shelly pushed her board over to them.

He glared at her. "This is your fault. You put her up to this."

Shelly widened her brown eyes. "Up to what? Learning to surf? Or pissing you off?"

He turned back to Lexie and realized he was making a colossal ass out of himself. Dropping Lexie's arm, he ran his hand through his hair. "I'm just saying that you don't know that man. He had his hands all over you. You're supposed to be in my custody."

Lexie's face tightened. "He's just teaching me to surf."

"Why didn't you ask me? I can teach you to surf." God, he was just mad. So damned mad. Why the hell did she let that man touch her like that? Worse, why did he care so damned much?

"It's not your job to teach me," she said calmly. She turned and headed back to the instructor, who was holding her board for her.

Nick stormed back to the shore. He was not going to stand there and watch another man pawing Lexie.

He went to the gym.

Lexie and Shelly had spent the day together, doing the spa and a little shopping at the resort boutique. She really couldn't afford all this, but Shelly had a discount and what the hell.

Okay, she wanted to look hot.

She slid the slinky black dress over a lacy thong, then she brushed out her hair to soft waves. With all the sun, she only needed a touch of makeup. After putting on her shoes, she looked at the time. Six thirty, time to check in with her PI. She sat on the bed, turned on her cell phone, and ignored the voice mail messages that were most likely from her family trying to make her call them.

Tate answered, "Hi, Lexie, no news."

He sounded frustrated. "Maybe he's given up." She'd liked Tate right away when she hired him. He was about her dad's age, a retired cop, and thorough.

"Maybe, but I'm worried. He should be frantic by now since he hasn't seen you. He should be making mistakes."

Her stomach clenched and tension shot up her spine, tightening her neck muscles. "He could have given up."

"I don't like the way this feels. Let me talk to your family. We need to clear up just how often your brother was in your apartment. He's not going in now, or I'd see him on the cameras I have set up."

She hesitated, not really wanting more trouble with her family. She knew Tate wanted to rule her brother out or see if he'd copied her house key, maybe given it to someone, but Lexie didn't think Larry would do that. Larry was about the opportunity—he wanted to have sex with a woman and obviously couldn't do it at home where his wife might catch him, so hey, why not use his sister's apartment. In his mind, that didn't hurt anyone. But giving out a copy of her house key would be dangerous; even Larry would know that.

Tate interrupted her thoughts. "This is your *life* we're talking about."

He was right. She cleared her throat and said, "Fine, do it." She gave him all the information he needed, all the while deciding that she had to move. She couldn't live in that apartment anymore. Just the idea of going back made her queasy. There was a knock on her door, so she said, "I'll call you tomorrow."

"Be careful."

She turned off her cell, checked the peephole, then answered the door. Shelly had on the silver dress she'd bought and looked fabulous.

"That dress ought to make Nick drool," Shelly said.

The black dress was fitted, low cut, and had a flared skirt for dancing. But between the phone call with her PI and thinking about Nick, her stomach was knotted and uneasy. "Maybe this isn't a good idea." Much as she liked Shelly, Lexie suspected that she and Mac were playing their own twisted version of matchmaker. She should stay out of it. Nick had his reasons and she should respect that.

But she'd given her impulsive streak a little

freedom, and now that streak was taking over. She was tired of being ignored—by her family and now by Nick. One second he acted like he cared, the next he told her she was just a job. It hurt more than it should, and she was lashing back by teasing him.

God, what did that make her?

Shelly snapped her fingers to get her attention. "We're going dancing, Lexie. I'm not letting you back out."

Lexie grabbed her purse and key card. "Okay," she agreed, because her only other option was to sit in her room and wonder where Nick was and worry about the stalker. They went across the resort to the Bayside Restaurant and Bar. As soon as they opened the door, they were blasted by the vibrant music with a salsa beat. Already five or six women were dancing with the hired male teachers, who were all yummy looking. They appeared to have a sultry Cuban or Spanish heritage. She looked around the bar, seeing several couples watching. There were a few stray men, either belonging to the women learning to dance, or perhaps hoping to score.

But no Nick. She told herself it was for the best.

An hour later, Lexie was hot and having fun. She'd danced with three of the male teachers and she totally sucked. She knew it, but she didn't care. The music was upbeat, the men were nice, the woman all laughed, and no one minded. No one judged; the whole point was just to have fun.

What a concept, no one judging her.

Raoul pulled her back against his chest and

said, "Try to follow me. It's supposed to be sexy."

She laughed. "I'm more comical than sexy."

"Not true." He settled his hands on her waist. "You're just self-conscious. Relax, let the music talk to your body."

Lexie closed her eyes to try, but the hair stood up on her arms.

"Having fun?"

Snapping her eyes open, she saw Nick. He towered over the other men. Wearing dark slacks, a cream-colored shirt rolled up his forearms, and a serious frown. "What are you doing here?"

Nick narrowed his eyes. "Came here to get a drink with Mac, and what do I find? You with another man's hands all over you." He moved in a step closer. "She's dancing with me." He glared over her shoulder at her dance partner.

Raoul lifted his hands off her waist. "Sure. Whatever."

"Nick!"

He looked down at her.

"Why are you doing this?" She was trying to keep her distance.

His jaw flexed hard enough to crack nuts.

Frustrated, she said, "Weren't you the one pushing me away?"

"I can't stop myself. Damn it, Lexie, you are turning me inside out." He leaned down. "You're making it impossible to do my job."

Her chest tightened. She was his job. He was pissed that he was sexually attracted to her when she was nothing more than a job. He was being forced into close proximity with her because she was in trouble.

A burden.

If she didn't do exactly as she was supposed to, then she was a burden. An inconvenience. A problem. She knew Nick had thought she'd be easy money. He'd counted on his charm to talk her into going back to Santa Barbara and he could collect his fee. Now he knew the truth: Lexie never did what she was supposed to. She always screwed things up.

The salsa music pulsed around her, escalating her anger until her fragile hold on her self-control shattered. Without a word, she dragged her arm away and slid past him. As soon as she reached the edge of the dance floor, she ran.

Out of the restaurant. Away from Nick. Away from the feelings he roused in her until she couldn't breathe. But she couldn't outrun her attraction to Nick—the man who didn't want to be attracted to her. She'd lain on top of him and felt his erection last night. Then he'd just pushed her away.

She hurried along the stone pathways, wondering where to go. Back to her room? Nick could find a way to get in there. And he had her car keys, damn it.

Where?

She kept going, winding around the stone paths down to the area called Palm Park. Swaying palm trees decorated with colored lights enclosed the small park. It had wrought iron tables and chairs with bright cushions surrounding a graceful dolphin fountain. Lexie followed the sound of the water. Colored lights shone up on the dolphin, illuminating the creature as he appeared to arch toward the sea. She could smell the ocean just yards away, but the little park was quiet. People had picnic lunches here or just sat and talked. Sometimes the park was rented out for weddings or parties.

Tonight the empty park echoed her loneliness. Sliding off her shoes, she set them on a bench and stepped into the water to ease the pain of dancing for an hour in high-heeled sandals.

She could probably strike dancer off her list of possible career choices.

"Lexie."

His tone was low, with an undertone of silky steel. It pissed her off that just his voice made her belly quiver. Holding out a hand to the gentle fall of water, she didn't look at him. "Take me back, Nick. Tonight. Get your money and we're done."

"Still being a martyr?"

She turned around, uncaring that the waterfall splashed her. "No. I'm being realistic. I'm done running. I'm going back." Her throat thickened as she stared at him. The blue, green, red, and yellow lights highlighted his inky black hair, the dark shadow on his clenched jaw, the breadth of his shoulders. He looked tense, ready to pounce. She forced herself to add, "Away from you. Either you take me and collect your money or I'll get there another way."

He stood as still as the statue except for his breathing, then he broke free, striding toward her.

He stopped at the edge of the fountain to kick off his shoes and pull off his socks. Then he stepped in and came face-to-face with her in two steps. "The hell you will. I'm not letting you go back when you're in danger."

It was all she could do not to back up. He was in her face, not touching her but close enough to feel his breath ruffle her hair. "It doesn't matter if I'm in danger. I'm just a job to you. Nothing more. No emotion involved. Do your job." She couldn't do it, couldn't stay with him one more minute constantly craving something from him he couldn't give her. She'd rather deal with her stalker. She'd find a way to ensure her safety. She could stay in a hotel if the cops didn't put her in jail.

He flexed his hands at his sides. "Be reasonable, Lexie."

The last thread of her control snapped. None of it mattered anymore. "I'm so damned tired of being reasonable. I ran away thinking my family would finally get it. They'd understand that I needed them for a change. Did that happen? No. And now I need you...and..." She shuddered and tears burned her eyes, ran down her face. Hot embarrassment flooded her. "I'm going back." She tried to turn, to get out of the water.

Nick caught her by the shoulders, his hands firm. He pushed her back a step, flush against the statue. His eyes caught the lights, flickering with a raw need. "I never let my lust get out of control. But you, Christ, you smash my willpower and make me ache for your touch. I'm done fighting. Hell with the consequences." He pressed his body into hers, his erection into her belly. "I'll worry about your safety tomorrow; tonight you're mine."

More tears brimmed over and ran hot down her face. "Nick." She put her arms around his neck.

He slammed his mouth down on hers, one hand sliding into her hair to hold her.

She inhaled the scent of him—soap and hot skin mixed with the water trickling over them. He made an impatient noise in his chest and invaded her mouth. Or she invaded his. She didn't know, and she didn't care, she just wanted Nick. Needed him to wrap himself around her and make her feel real and substantial. She slid her tongue along his and dug her fingers into his shoulders. Hot desire ripped through her.

Nick slid his hand off her shoulder and cupped her breast, squeezing just enough. She moved against him. He ran the pad of his thumb over her pebbled nipple through the thin dress, making her shiver. She stroked her hand over the soft material of his shirt, down the front of his pants, and pressed her palm against his dick.

He groaned deep in his chest. Lifting his head, he said, "What are you wearing under the dress?"

She rasped out, "Panties. Thong."

He slid both his hands down the sides of her body, dropping to his knees. "Show me."

She looked at him on his knees in the water, his pants getting wet, his head tilted as he stared up at her with those eyes. He put his hands on the outside of her knees. "Now."

Lexie pulled up her dress until she felt the cool air and wet spray from the waterfall.

Nick dropped his gaze. "Damn." He stroked his hands up her thighs, over the thong, then grasped the edge and eased it down and off. Then he reached up and pressed her legs apart. The cool mist touched her sex and she shivered.

"God. I've wanted this." He slid his thumbs along her seam, and parted her folds to spread her beneath his gaze. After a few seconds, he touched her clitoris, stroking his thumb in intoxicating circles around the aching bud.

Lexie fell back against the statue, her back wet, the dress sticking to her while she held up the skirt. "Nick..."

"I'm not stopping. Not now."

She saw his dark head lean into her thighs, then his tongue touched her, sliding over her clit and deeper to taste all of her. A shudder wracked her.

Nick reached up one hand to hold her against the statue.

He centered his tongue on her clit, wet, lapping circles until Lexie thought she'd cry. She ground against him, desperate. "Oh!"

He increased his licks and slid his hand deep between her legs, one finger easing inside her.

Panting, she knew she was making noise. Probably begging. Nothing had ever felt like this. Free. Sexy. Just her and Nick. The cold water on her skin, her dress wet against her sensitive breasts, and Nick sucking her, thrusting his finger in her.

Then he added a second finger. Lexie shattered,

her entire body rocking with deep spasms of pleasure. Nick pushed her further, tonguing her, thrusting his fingers inside her to keep her orgasm going until she was breathless.

He rose up, his eyes so light with gold, they were intense. "Keep holding that dress." He undid his pants and pulled his cock out.

In the colored lights, his penis looked deep in color, thick and long. She had never wanted to be filled up like she did now.

Tonight. By Nick. She might have whimpered.

"Every time you make that noise, it makes me hornier." Gripping her bottom, he effortlessly lifted her up, and held her against the wet column of the statue. "Take me, Lexie."

"Are you sure? It slippery in here and—" Suddenly her eyes widened. "Condoms."

"Shit." He eased her down to her feet.

Chapter 6

NICK INSERTED THE KEYCARD, OPENED the door, and looked at Lexie.

The flush of her orgasm was fading from her face. Her dress was wet and clinging to her breasts and legs. He had her panties in his hand with his shoes and socks. She shivered as she walked into the air-conditioned room.

No way was he letting her think too much. He was light-years past thinking and one hundred percent into Lexie, just Lexie. Shutting the door, he tossed the stuff he carried, took the shoes from her hand, and rubbed her shoulders and bare arms. He felt her tremble, felt the rise of gooseflesh beneath his palms. "I only want you wet where I make you wet. And shivering when I make you shiver." He moved behind her and found the zipper of her dress. Dropping a kiss on her shoulder, he slid the zipper down her long back, then pushed the tiny straps down her arms. The material whispered down her body, revealing her tan lines, the white swells of her ass, her legs. He reached to gather her in his arms and remembered his wet clothes.

Nick stripped off his clothes. Then he pulled her against him. Her skin against his, her curves pressing against him. He leaned down to her neck, inhaling the scent of her, the lingering sunscreen, slight chlorine of the waterfall water, and just pure Lexie. He could still taste her on his tongue. Unable to stop from touching her, he skimmed his hands over her nipples, feeling the tremor go through her. Cupping her breasts, he brushed his thumbs back and forth across her nipples. His cock strained against her back. "I want you, the real you. Raw, honest, riding my cock, Lexie. Taking the pleasure you crave. The pleasure you denied yourself trying to be good and perfect for everyone else."

She leaned back into him. "Yes."

It ripped through him, the untainted trust in her. She'd been riding the edge of wild since he'd met her, reaching for a chance to throw off the shackles but always pulling back. No pulling back tonight. Not with him. He'd known in that first kiss, when she'd melted into him with trust, that she'd let go for him.

It had scared him to death.

Now his cock thickened and his pulse pounded. He glided his hand down her belly, sensitive to the quivers in her stomach muscles. Dipping between her legs, he separated her gently. She was soft and wet, her body opening to him. Male pride swelled and drove him to give her pleasure, to push her to be free with him. He stroked her, and she writhed against him, her skin sliding over his while his fingers sank into her wet heat. She arched against him, forcing his fingers deeper into her body.

He groaned. "Condom," he told her. Taking his hands off her body, he went to his dresser and found the condoms. Grabbing one, he turned and holy God, he stopped. Lexie's hair was wild, her face flushed, her eyes sparkling. Her breasts were tightly nubbed, and between her legs, her curls were wet. Her clit peeked out.

She came to him, taking the condom, opening it, and sliding it on him.

He grabbed her shoulders, pushed her back to the bed, and went down on top of her. Nick opened his mouth over hers, sucking her tongue. He was so hard, so goddamned desperate to be inside her, he worried he'd hurt her. Grabbing her waist, he rolled her over him. "Let me watch you."

She rose up on her knees and straddled him, her hair sliding over her shoulders and brushing over her tits. Taking hold of his cock, she pressed the tip against her sleek, hot entry. She was looking down, watching as he slid partway into her. Then she looked up at him.

He reached over his head, hooking his fingers around the wrought iron headboard. "More, Lexie. Jesus, you're killing me." Her walls were hot and slick and sucking him in. Sweat coated him. But he caught the flare in her brown eyes begging for him to help her lose control. To shed that tight leash of responsibility and seize what she craved. "Take it, Lexie. You want it, take it."

She bore down on him, swallowing his cock into her tight sheath.

Nick squeezed his fingers around the wrought iron over his head. The feel of her body taking him in deep slammed him with a truth—this wasn't just sex, but an all-consuming passion.

Lexie began to move, sliding him in and out, torturing the hell out of him. The need to possess and fill her until she came so hard, she'd never forget him grew, but he fought to let her set the pace. Color rose in her face and chest, and she began to undulate in a frantic way.

Nick got it, realized what she was trying for. He let go of the headboard, reaching down to separate her folds and expose her clit.

She stopped moving, startled.

He looked into her face, desperate to reassure her. To teach her to take what she needed from him. "I want to feel you rubbing your pussy on me while my cock is deep inside you." He took hold of her hips, showing her how to rock herself on him.

She caught on and took over, her face glowing as she pleasured herself on his body. The sight drove him right to the edge of losing his mind. God. He arched up under her, grabbing the headboard as she rode him. Her breasts bounced, her face tightened, and she arched as she found it...her orgasm.

She made sexy noises, bearing down on him, rubbing her pleasure on him. Her face flooded with color, and Jesus, she was so fucking beautiful.

He lost it. He reared up to put his arm around

her shoulders and pulled her onto his chest. He had to feel her, hold her. Putting his free hand on her lower back, he dug his heels into the bed and thrust up high and hard. Her body was soft and pliant and he couldn't get enough of her. He thrust harder, deeper.

A small voice warned, *Don't hurt her.*

But he went deeper and came holding Lexie against his chest, feeling her hot skin against his and inhaling her scent.

As soon as he could breathe, he said, "Did I hurt you?"

A small tremor went through her, wrapping around his cock. "No."

He knew it was true. Her body was spread out, still soft and supple, with little aftershocks of pleasure. He hadn't hurt her. He'd just lost control.

And his mind.

Lexie watched the cold gray dawn, barely able to see the ocean. She could just make out the white caps of the waves. Fog chilled her and she wrapped both hands around her mug of coffee. The noise of the crashing waves somehow sounded like freedom to her. Like the powerful sense of freedom she'd felt last night.

She hoped the sound of the waves would always remind her of that precious feeling. And of Nick.

She knew last night cost him, blurred lines that he couldn't emotionally afford to blur. Ellen's murder haunted him, and he coped by keeping sex and duty separate. Who was she to judge that? Hadn't she been judged enough? She wouldn't do that to Nick. One day, he would find a woman he could care about again. A woman who came without trouble that brought out the memories for him.

Hearing the slide of the door behind her, she tried not to tense up.

Nick moved up behind her. "What are you doing out here? Can't you sleep?"

"I didn't mean to wake you."

He reached around her, sliding the cup from her hands to take a drink, then settling the warm mug between her palms. He wrapped her in his arms. "You're cold. Come back to bed."

She had put on his shirt because it was easier than her dress. His warmth penetrated the material and she could feel his hard-on pressing against her lower back. Desire rose, thick and desperate. But with the morning came the consequences. "No. We should get going. It's a long drive."

His arms tightened around her. "Lexie."

She turned, stepping out of his hold and putting a little distance between them. "I'm not going to let you bend your rules because of some kind of twisted logic that you have to protect me. You don't. I'll handle this situation with the stalker. I'll go back and fix things."

"You mean cave in to your family?"

There was enough light now for her to see Nick wearing only his boxers. She intimately knew the curve of his shoulders, the feel of his muscles covered by skin that smelled like Nick—bold and determined. He was powerful and overwhelming as a lover, and yet, she'd touched a part of him last night that was vulnerable. He handled his vulnerability by keeping barriers in place; she wasn't going to cross those barriers and cause him more pain.

"I'll deal with it, Nick. They're my family, and all I have. I shouldn't have run."

He returned her stare. "Running was the first smart thing you did." Dragging a hand through his hair, he added, "I read some of your book. You're good. It's only Wednesday. We have until Friday morning. Keep working on your book."

Her chest hollowed, and her hands tingled like they were falling asleep. She set the coffee cup down on the small table. "You looked at my book? On my laptop?" It was hers. Her book. Just hers. The only thing she had that was hers. Emotions welled up, burned. Anger? Nerves? Did he like it? She didn't know what she felt.

"Yes. You fell asleep while working on it the night we went to Mac and Shelly's. I was making sure the file was saved to shut down your computer...and I ended up reading. I'm not sorry, Lex. I read for hours. I didn't want to stop. Hell, I've been trying to work up the courage to ask you to read the rest of it."

She stepped farther back, hit the edge of the chair, and fought for her balance. Something was moving inside her, shifting and swelling.

Nick closed his hand around her arm. "I know it

was wrong to invade your privacy. But where you're concerned, I have no self-control. None." He voice dropped to a caress. "I like you in my shirt."

She shivered and couldn't resist asking, "You liked it? The book?"

"Yes." He pulled her against him, leaned down, and kissed her.

She couldn't sort it all out, but Nick wrapped one arm around her waist, lifted her up, and carried her inside. Taking her mouth from his, she tried to keep the boundaries in place. "Sex? This is about vacation sex, right?"

His grin turned wicked. "Sun, sand, and sex. Mostly sex." He tossed her on the bed.

She had to be out of her mind. He had the ability to keep his emotions separate, but she knew it was too late for her anyway. She cared for Nick, cared so much she couldn't leave him and yet was desperate to ease his worries and conscience. Did two more days really matter? Bouncing on the bed where he tossed her, she watched him strip off his boxers. He was hard, his dick thick and twitching. Still wearing his shirt, she got to her knees on the mattress and touched his hard shaft.

He thrust his hips and groaned at her touch. Sinking his hand in her hair, he tilted her head up to him and said, "I intended to go slow, drive you crazy—"

She cut him off. "Nick?" He closed his eyes as she stroked his cock and cupped his balls.

"What?" He groaned.

"Shut up and get down to business."

He snapped his eyes open. A slow, wicked grin spread over his mouth. He reached out and slid his shirt halfway down her arms, then he picked her up and settled her on her back.

Lexie realized he'd bared her body to him, but trapped her arms to her sides. She could roll over and free herself, but why the heck would she do that? She pretended to protest just for the fun of it. "No fair."

He laughed, then he bent her legs, spread her knees, and looked his fill. After a long minute, he glided a finger around her clit, teasing the bud until she swelled and throbbed. The aching need bloomed, making her writhe. Without a shred of self-consciousness, she spread her thighs, giving him access. That was the danger of Nick, with him she didn't want to hold anything back.

He took his hand away.

"Don't stop." It came out a breathless demand.

He went to the dresser and got a condom. "Lexie?"

She watched him roll the condom onto himself. "Hmm?"

"Shut up, sweetheart." He lowered his body to cover hers, all his heat and male hardness pressing her into the mattress. His cockhead pressed against her entrance, and eased in an inch, then he paused to stare down at her. "Unless you're whimpering for more." He thrust hard, reaching the spot that fired her nerves. A spot only he knew.

She whimpered, wrapped her legs around him, and arched up to take more of him.

"Or panting." He thrust again.

Her breath rushed out of her.

Nick rose up, placing his arms on either side of her head. He looked down at her, his eyes golden. "Or you come..." He slammed into her, over and over, deeper. "Come hard, Lexie, squeeze me."

She cried out, her release pulsing and squeezing even as he shoved her halfway up the bed, burying his cock in her and groaning his release.

Nick rolled her over on top of him and stripped the shirt off her, throwing it to the side. Then his arms wrapped around her, holding her. He drew one hand down her back to spread his fingers over her butt cheek. "How about you spend the day writing in bed while naked?"

Lexie sank into his warmth, hearing the slam of her heart, feeling the sting of his sweat against her face. Her whole body throbbed. "I think you tricked me into staying under false pretenses, bounty hunter." She took a breath and asked, "Will you be naked too?"

He tightened his arm around her. "Oh, yeah."

Chapter 7

LEXIE'S STOMACH RUMBLED LOUDLY.

Nick walked out of the bathroom with a towel slung around his hips. "Is that your subtle way of telling me to feed you?"

She laughed. "A body can't exist on sex alone." Although she was happy enough to try. He looked good in a towel. It was a shame to watch him pull on board shorts.

The room phone rang, startling her.

Nick walked over and grabbed it. "Vardolous." A pause, then, "Yes, she's here." He handed her the phone.

"It's for me?" Who could possibly know she was in Nick's room?

Nick grinned. "It's Mac."

She took the phone, a little bemused. "Hi, Mac, is something wrong?"

"Evidently not, if you're in Nick's room."

She blushed, remembering breakfast with Mac and Shelly yesterday morning. Lexie had known they were doing some creative matchmaking. "Uh, what can I do for you?"

"Can you come up to the lobby for a few minutes?"

"Why?" She had no idea why he'd want to see her.

"Nothing to worry about. The resort manager would just like a quick minute."

Was something wrong with her credit card? She wasn't anywhere near her limit. "Uh, okay. I'll be there in a few minutes."

"See you then." Mac hung up.

Lexie set the phone down and stared at it.

Nick walked up behind her, and rubbed his hands over her bare arms. "What's up?"

She turned. "The resort manager wants to see me. I don't know why. I'm sure my credit card is fine. I haven't done anything wrong."

He laughed. "Why don't we stop by your room so you can get your swimsuit and laptop, then we'll go see what terrible crime you've committed. If you aren't arrested, we can get some breakfast, and I was thinking that maybe you'd like to try surfing again before you get to work."

"You mean the class?" She'd had fun in the class except when Nick got all bent out of shape.

His dark eyebrows drew together in a frown. "Not a chance. It'll be my hands all over you this morning." Drawing himself up, he added, "I'll teach you."

She didn't get it. "Why?"

He stroked his fingertips over her cheek and

along her jaw with a possessive touch. "Because when you stood up on the surfboard yesterday, I could see your smile even from a distance. I want to see it again. You were doing pretty good. Come on, it'll be fun."

He wanted her to have fun. With him. She was just digging herself in deeper and deeper. "Well, uh—"

He leaned down, brushing his mouth over hers. "Or we can come back to my room and you can try to work naked."

Shivers danced in her stomach, but she tried to form a stern expression. "Try? I'm very serious about my book, I'll have you know."

"Hmm. I might have to test the level of your commitment."

He dropped a hand to the bare skin of her thigh and slid it under her dress.

God, she was too easy when it came to Nick. She wanted to yank off her dress, strip off his board shorts, and...she shoved him away. "Hands off, bounty hunter. Mac is expecting me soon."

Lazy mischief darkened his eyes. "I could kill him and solve the problem."

"Nick!" Her horror somehow turned into laughter. There was nothing sexier than a man making her feel desired. Nick had that way about him. *With all women?* she wondered. That thought hurt, but Lexie was determined to accept that this was just vacation sex, nothing more. "Let's go."

Since she had showered in Nick's room, it didn't take her long to put on her bathing suit and cover-up, then grab her beach bag. They left their laptops in her room for now and walked to the lobby. It was cool inside with the lazy ceiling fans, mosaic tiles, and an indoor waterfall. Mac strode toward them with two women, both wearing the blue and white resort colors.

Mac grinned at her. "Lexie, I'd like you to meet the resort manager, Rose, and our event coordinator, Vivian."

Rose had short blond hair and a wide smile. "Hi, Lexie, Mac's told us a lot about you. So has the staff that has worked with you to book rooms for your clients' honeymoons."

At a loss for what to do, Lexie smiled and said, "It's a pleasure to meet both of you. What can I do for you?" The professional tone was automatic, although she felt awkward in her bikini and flip-flops. What did they want? She was pretty sure it had nothing to do with My Perfect Wedding.

Rose said, "I'll make this quick so you can make the most of a beautiful day here at our resort. Vivian will be leaving Sand Castle Resort in a month. I understand that you are an excellent wedding planner but you're considering a career change. I've talked to two of your clients this morning, and they raved about you. I'd like you to consider a job as an event coordinator here at Sand Castle."

She turned and looked at Mac.

His blue eyes glittered. "I recommended you, and the staff backed me up."

A vein of possibility opened up, spilling out

JENNIFER LYON

excitement. She could move to San Diego, work at the resort, and write in her spare time. It'd be a fresh start, put some distance between her and her demanding family. She'd have to plan some weddings, but she'd also be planning events for businesses. It'd be different and challenging. She already had friends—Shelly and Mac. Her mind spun, trying to break it down and grasp it.

Nick checked her thoughts when he said, "She can't work here. She lives in Santa Barbara."

The excitement drained out like her lifeblood. San Diego was Nick's home. Mac and Shelly were his friends. Lexie didn't belong here, she was just...vacation sex. She turned back to Rose and Vivian. "Thank you. I'm pleased that you would consider me. But I won't be able to accept."

Rose's sharp gaze drifted over all of them, then settled on Lexie. "I'm sure the offer is a surprise. Why don't you take some time to think it over? We can talk later." She reached out her hand.

Lexie shook it and turned to shake Vivian's hand. To be polite, she said, "That's very generous of you. I'll be in touch with you soon."

Nick watched Lexie ride her third wave of the morning, his chest swelling with pride in her. She was a great student, willing to listen to direction, yet trusting her own body. She didn't try to fight the waves, she let them carry her and the board. When she fell off the last wave, he swam to her. She popped up with a proud smile.

He pulled her into his arms and kissed her.

She leaned back, still grinning. "That was so cool!"

"You're a natural."

She smiled at him. "Thanks, Nick. I really had fun, and you're a good teacher. I'm ready to go in, though. I want to work for a while."

He grabbed the board. "All right." They made their way to the shore and their cabana. While Lexie settled in, Nick went to the room and collected both their laptops. He could get a little work done too.

They both booted up their machines and focused on their projects.

A few minutes later, Nick was reading an e-mail from his lawyer about the partnership papers with Mac when Lexie said, "Nick, I copied my book, if, you know, you still want to read it. Here."

He looked up to see her holding out a flash drive.

"I mean, if you don't want to read it, fine. I just thought..."

Her brown eyes had such hope and fear it made him forget to breathe. He reached out and took the flash drive. "I can read it? I know I didn't ask the first time, but I'm asking now."

She shrugged. "If you want to. Or not. Doesn't matter to me."

It mattered. He could see it in the lines of her tense arms, raised shoulder, and strained neck. "I want to." He shifted his laptop and got up, then he leaned over and kissed her. "Thank you. I know how much this book means to you."

She stared at him with wide eyes, grateful excitement and something else—a sweet caring—gleaming in the brown depths. "I'm not being that brave. By next week, I'll never see you again. Even if you hate it, what do I have to lose?"

He kissed her again to shut her up. The thought of her being gone from his life lingered. And he didn't like it, not one damned bit.

But he'd get used to it. He always did. Nick loaded the flash drive and started reading.

It was past lunchtime when Lexie stood. "I'm going to cool off in the water." He waved her away, then watched her walk down the sand toward the waves. Her black bikini cupped her ass in a way that made his hands curl with the need to feel her butt in his palms. He dragged his gaze from her and back to reading.

Until Mac's voice intruded. "What's the word, Vardolous?"

"Scram." He didn't look up, too involved in the story to tolerate interruptions from his long-time friend.

"Who's that man Lexie is talking to?"

Nick looked up.

Mac laughed. "You're so predictable."

He glared at the other man. "Why haven't I killed you?"

Mac's gaze grew serious. "Because I'm your business partner."

Nick rubbed his eyes with his thumb and forefinger. He and Mac had already leased a building for the karate studio. Nick wasn't backing out, but he liked screwing with Mac's abundant confidence. "I haven't signed the papers yet."

"You will. You're tired of the nomad life and you know it."

Uncomfortable at how easily Mac read him, he shifted the subject. "I know you and Shelly were goading Lexie into driving me crazy."

"Good times, huh?"

Leaning his head back, he stared out at the waves where Lexie stood waist deep in the water. "You went too far with the job offer. You're sticking your nose where it doesn't belong." It would be hard enough when he left Lexie in Santa Barbara. But having her in San Diego? Close by? How would he stay away from her?

"I know this will come as a shock to your enormous ego, but the job offer isn't about you. It's about Lexie. Shelly and I like her."

Nick narrowed his gaze. "You never chummed up with the other women I slept with."

"You didn't bring them around."

He hadn't wanted to bring them around. They were nice women, but he hadn't been interested in introducing them to his friends or family. Lexie had met his mom and sister, and his friends. He was losing control of this situation. "I didn't bring them around because you obviously fancy yourself a matchmaker."

"Nah. Don't have time since I'm going into partnership with you. And I plan to kick your ass regularly. In front of students."

Nick considered that. "Yeah? How about I kick

your ass right now in front of all the people at the beach?"

Mac snorted. "It's not snowing in hell, so it's not happening."

Nick had taken down vicious animals masquerading as men many times as a bounty hunter, but Mac was formidable as a sparring opponent. He had a fourth-degree black belt in karate, and that was only one of his disciplines. There was no one he'd rather have at his back. Mac was fast.

Nick was power. And a sixth-degree black belt.

Mac stood. "Just checking in. Want to have dinner with us tonight? Maybe take the girls dancing?"

His gut twisted. "Girls? I'm not dating Lexie, we're just having sex. She's not *my girl*." It sounded like high school, for Christ's sake, not a mature decision to slake their lust.

"Well, I am a girl. Sheesh. Hi, Mac." Lexie lifted up her laptop and dropped into the chair.

Christ, his timing sucked. "Sorry, I just meant—"

She waved her hand at him. "Guy talk, I know. Go with Mac and Shelly tonight. Have fun." Lexie shoved her wet hair out of her face and opened her computer like he wasn't even there.

What the hell? He sat up. "What's that supposed to mean?"

"Uh, I have to go...work or something." Mac turned and strolled off, whistling.

Nick ignored him to stare at Lexie.

She met his gaze. "Mac's just messing with you. I

know that. Don't worry about it. I'll see you when you get back."

"Back from where?" What the hell was wrong with her? She was acting irrational.

She widened her eyes. "Dinner, dancing, whatever you're doing. I thought that's what Mac said."

Her guileless expression shafted him with a streak of guilt. He ran his hand over the back of his neck, feeling the bulge of his tense muscles. It wasn't her acting like an ass, it was him. And that bastard Mac kept setting him up to say stupid things in front of Lexie. "Look, if you want to go dancing, we'll go."

Her brown eyes dropped to her laptop. "Don't be ridiculous. I never said I wanted to go dancing with you."

That stung and pushed him right back into pissed off again. "You were happy enough to dance with all those men last night. Now you don't want to dance with me? What's wrong with me?"

"Maybe you've been out in the sun too long?"

He leaned back in his chair and looked down at the laptop. "I'm not the one who's being unreasonable." He started reading and ignored her. He didn't want to think about this...anger, frustration and okay, yeah, regret churning inside him. He couldn't concentrate because he kept seeing the days ahead without Lexie. And he didn't like the view. Staring at the words, he said, "It's just that we aren't in a relationship. We only have a couple days."

She resumed typing on her book. "Sun, sand, and sex. I know. Not a problem."

Good. He read a sentence, but it didn't make any sense. This was her fault. Did she have to be so damned cheerful about it? Didn't the sex mean anything? How many men made her come like he did?

He didn't want to know.

He needed a beer. An ice-cold beer. Standing up, he said, "Want anything from the bar?"

"Iced tea or anything cold. Thanks."

He stood there staring down at her, watching her gnaw at her lower lip as she thought about something while staring at the computer. Her hair was drying into a stringy mess, her face was free of all makeup, and yet, she looked pretty. Real.

She looked up, then flushed. "Oh, sorry. I know I have my room key here somewhere to pay for the drink."

Caught staring at her like a love struck puppy—which he wasn't—he jerked his gaze away and snatched up his room key. "I'll buy the damned drinks." He stalked off, got the drinks and returned to the cabana. Setting the drinks on the table, he picked up the computer and settled in to read the book.

"Thanks. I'll buy the next round."

He refused to let her bait him. No woman had ever turned him into a stark raving butthead before. Not even Ellen. Ellen had made him feel needed, powerful and strong. Lexie made him crazy. The kind of crazy that drove him to act like a

Neanderthal, just as Shelly had accused him of being. He wanted to claim her as his and kill anyone else who looked at her.

Sunstroke was a distinct possibility.

The best thing to do was just shut the hell up. He probably shouldn't look at her again either since he seemed to have a little staring problem too. Best to let her think anything she liked, even believe that he was a total jerk. But he was not taking money from her. No way would he leech off her like her family. He'd buy her damned drinks. Hell, he'd buy her dinner, take her dancing, and if he stayed near her too much longer, he might buy her a car and house.

It had to be sunstroke. Or heat stroke. Something was definitely wrong with him. He turned his full attention back to the book.

After reading the same sentence six more times, it finally dawned on him why it wasn't making sense. It didn't fit. And it was in bold print, standing out from the rest of the words on the page. His heart sped up, and he sat forward to read.

You have a secret life writing your book. I have a secret life, a life THEY will never control. We're meant to be together, in spite of THEM. Together in our secret love.

Wait for me, I'll fulfill your craving for adventure.

Nick went back over what Lexie had told him in his head. She thought the stalker had left her laptop on. Jesus Christ. "Lexie."

"Hmm." She kept typing.

"Do you reread your work? Or do you just keep going forward?"

"Depends, why?" Frowning, she looked up at him. Her eyes were shadowed, but he saw her shoulders tense. "I told you it was rough. Typos and—"

He softened. "This isn't about typos. Please, Lex, just answer me. Have you gone back and read through your book?"

"No. Not since about the halfway point. I want to get to the end, then rewrite. Why? What's the problem?"

He looked around and could have kicked his own ass. It was midafternoon and there were tons of people milling around. "I don't want you to get upset, but I found something that doesn't seem to belong in your book."

She stared at him. "Like an unnecessary scene?"

"No." He got up and walked around to her with his computer.

She pushed her computer down her thighs to make room for his machine.

Nick set it down and pointed with his finger to the passage he'd found buried in her work.

Lexie quietly read it, then said, "Oh God. Nick, I didn't write that."

He hunkered down by her chair and put his hand on her shoulder. "No, I didn't think so." He felt a tremor go through her. Rubbing her shoulder, he looked into her eyes. "Let's pack up and go to the room. We'll talk there."

Lexie found a second note embedded in the manuscript, in bold print.

Danger is an aphrodisiac. You feel it, Lexie, the danger of never knowing when I'll show up. What will I do to you? Maybe you'll be in the shower...maybe you'll be in your bed...just make sure you're alone. You belong to me, only me.

A dirty, greasy feeling roiled in her stomach. She'd poured her heart into the book, into a thriller with a heroine who had to rise to incredible challenges, and yeah, there was sex, but... "Oh God, he's making it disgusting, he's..."

"A twisted prick." Nick put his arm around her shoulders. "There's nothing wrong with your book. It's him twisting things in his perverted head."

She copied and pasted the passage for the file they were going to send to her PI, Tate. Nick had talked to him on the phone, so he was waiting.

She kept searching. It looked like the stalker had put his comments in bold so she could find them. The ring of the room phone interrupted her. "Maybe it's Tate." She got up, walking over the cold tile to circle the bed and grab the phone. "Hello."

Silence, then, "So Larry was right. While your mother is working herself into another heart attack, you're on vacation."

"Dad?" She began to shake, needing her father. Staring at the textured green walls of her room, she struggled to get control of herself. "Is Mom okay? Did she have another heart attack?"

"You've had your fun. Get back here and help

your mother. Larry and Amber are making her nuts, she's screaming at everyone. You know she's sick. Stop acting like a child."

Her eyes filled with tears, and the green walls blurred. "Dad—"

Nick startled her by grabbing the phone from her hand. "Mr. Rollins—"

Lexie experienced a wave of sheer relief, a second where she could just breathe. Then she got a hold of herself. This was her father. She reached over and snatched the phone back, determined to take control. "Dad—"

"You're with a man? While your mother—"

"Stop it!" It felt surprisingly good to fight back. "Stop trying to guilt me into fixing everything. Mom is fine, the doctor assured us of that. If you want Amber and Larry to back off, tell them yourself. You and Mom allowed them to leech off you, so you can put an end to it." She wouldn't cry anymore, damn it. She refused to look at Nick, although she could feel him staring at her. Instead, she kept her gaze on the green mosaic tile.

Her dad said, "Of all the selfish—"

Nick put his arm around her and pulled her into his side, but he didn't try to take the phone from her again. He just stood next to her like an anchor. It gave Lexie strength. Calmly, she said, "No, I'm not being selfish. I'm scared, Dad. More scared than I've ever been. I needed you, but you wouldn't listen to me."

"Is this that stalker thing again? Look, Larry admitted that he was in your apartment with a girl.

He knows it was wrong. You have no business sending that private investigator to talk to him. What if his wife had found out?"

She leaned against Nick. "Good to know where your priorities are, Dad." She bent over and set the phone down. Emotion welled up and tightened her throat, but she wasn't going to fall apart. She was a woman, not a child. She would take care of herself and be fine.

The phone rang.

She ignored it and went to the computer. "Don't answer it. I have nothing else to say to him."

"Your decision." Nick sat next to her. "Want to talk about that shit with your brother?"

She assumed he had been able to hear her dad on the phone. "He screwed his girlfriend in my apartment. In the beginning I assumed the stuff I found was Larry's doing. We had a huge fight. He had stolen the key to my apartment from my mom. I made him give it back. It was ugly. He told my parents that he made a mistake and was trying to fix his marriage. He also claimed that I was trying to ruin his marriage because I was jealous." She paged down the manuscript, looking for the next note from the stalker.

Nick said, "Your brother is an asshole."

"I know. But he's the son my dad always wanted. Whatever." She paged down to the next section in her book and froze.

Each time I check and see that you've been working on your book, I know you're staying home at night. Being a good girl and

waiting for me. When I'm here in your apartment, I am too hard to wait. Have to take the edge off. You have such pretty underwear... Today I left the bed unmade for you. Lie there and know I was there...And I'll be back.

She was going to throw up. She'd slept in her bed after...

Nick shoved his chair back and turned Lexie so she was facing the bed. He reached up behind her and forced her head down toward her knees. "Breathe. In and out."

She did what he told her, fighting to force the refrigerated air in and out of her lungs. The black spots dancing in front of her eyes started to fade and her nausea eased up. Finally she said, "I'm okay."

He took his hand off the back of her neck.

Sitting up, she studied Nick. His face was pulled tight to reveal his prominent cheekbones and blazing eyes.

He said, "There might be more."

She shook her head. "There's not."

"Lexie..."

"There's not. I came home from work one day and saw my laptop opened on my unmade bed. From then on, I took it with me to work." She forced herself to breathe and fight not to let the nausea rise. "I thought it was Larry. Bringing his girlfriend to my apartment, then checking his e-mail. Or that they were reading my book and making fun of me." She hadn't been able to believe some unknown person was getting into her apartment. It hadn't seemed real or possible.

Nick took her hand. "Okay, let's send all this to Tate. Maybe he can get a lead. But first I need to ask one thing."

She knew what he was going to ask. "I don't know who it is, Nick. Nothing rings a bell. I haven't dated in months. I just don't know." Damn it, she wouldn't cry. She had to think. What should she do next? "Do we go back now?"

"Hell no. Tate's an ex-cop, and he and I know some of the same cops in Santa Barbara. We'll ask Tate to file a report with them and get the process started. But we don't know who the stalker is, Lexie. All the police will do is open a file. We need some kind of break to point the police in the right direction."

She fought hard to stay in control. She didn't ever want to go back to Santa Barbara. She wanted to stay here in the room with Nick. Forever. But that wasn't reality. She had to go back, face the charges against her and deal with the stalker.

Nick had his own life to get back to.

Chapter 8

"DO YOU THINK IT COULD be your brother behind this?" Tate asked over the speakerphone.

Lexie felt both Nick and Mac look at her. They were using Mac's office. Mac sat behind his desk across from them, while Nick sat on her right. She had her laptop on the desk in case Tate needed anything else off it. She wasn't sure how to answer.

Did she think it could be Larry?

She felt ill just considering it. "That's not really Larry's style. He's not likely to put so much effort into something like this. Plus he relies on me to fix his screwups."

Tate said, "He seems really angry at you. He denied making a copy of your mom's key to your apartment before giving it back, but I think he's lying."

"Probably," she agreed, done with pretending about her family. "That's just like Larry. Tuck a key away in case another opportunity for a little adultery comes up."

"Could he be trying to discredit you so that his wife and your parents don't believe you?" Tate asked.

Her stomach tightened painfully. "About using my apartment for an affair?"

"Yes."

"He might, except that Larry's brain doesn't work that way. He's reactive, not proactive. He doesn't think ahead, that's why I have to double-check every cake order, remind him where and when the cakes need to be delivered. I could see where he might write one note, but..." She shook her head while keeping her gaze fixed on her computer screen. "Copying my mom's key to my apartment is about as far ahead as he thinks. He simply had the opportunity—saw my key at Mom's and swiped it. Then he had it, so why not copy it? But coming up with and following through on a plan to discredit me is too involved for him."

Tate said, "Okay. Anyone else? I've checked out the two men you gave me who were odd. Both of them seem to be in the clear."

Nick looked over at her and raised a questioning eyebrow.

She explained, "One was the father of a bride and the other a best man. I thought they were long shots."

Tate explained, "I told Lexie to tell me anyone who seemed interested in her, no matter how remote a possibility it seemed."

Mac surprised her by jumping in with, "What about the guy you stapled?"

Lexie lifted her head. "William Harry Livingston?" She frowned. "The cops told me he's a respectable guy and never been in any trouble."

Nick sat up next to her. "You suspected him? Lexie?"

She twisted her fingers. "After the note on my car, I was scared. I probably jumped to conclusions."

"Don't forget the underwear. That kind of behavior is a sign of a dangerous stalker."

"What underwear?" Nick said.

She winced at his harsh tone. "I told you some underwear was missing. Well, it turned up with that note."

Tate added, "The underwear had been hacked up into little pieces and stuffed in a Ziploc bag. It was left with the note on her car."

"Jesus Christ!" Nick exploded to his feet and glared down at her. "Why didn't you tell me?"

"Because the police found my fingerprints on the Ziploc bag and the stationery." She would never forget the visit from the detective. They thought she was a whack job looking for attention or trying to get out of the assault charge. She crossed her arms over her stomach, trying to just hold on. Or shield herself from Nick if he didn't believe her.

"Nick, calm down," Mac said.

He ignored Mac to stare at her. "You should have told me."

A throbbing started behind her eyes. "I didn't want you to take me back to Santa Barbara."

He snorted. "I'm not your asshole brother, Lexie. I believe you. Obviously the stalker took one of your

Ziploc bags and your stationery when he was in your apartment."

Stunned, she lifted her gaze to him. He just believed her? No explanations, no battle? It was that simple? The thing that had been shifting and moving inside her for days slid and locked into place.

She was in love with Nick.

And she was so screwed.

Nick turned from her and said to the speakerphone, "Tate, we need to find out who is powerful enough to make the cops believe Lexie is doing this to herself. Cops aren't stupid, they wouldn't just believe anyone."

Tate answered, "Right there with you. I'm going to start running more in-depth backgrounds on everyone Lexie gave me. So far I haven't found any trail, but I just haven't picked at the right thread yet."

Lexie took a deep breath. "William Harry Livingston, Tate. Start with him."

"Why?" Nick and Tate said it at the same time.

"Because his mother is a judge." She had completely forgotten. "Harry is a mild man, about five foot eight, maybe one hundred and fifty pounds. He's a real estate agent. I only met his mother at the rehearsal dinner. Otherwise, she had nothing to do with the wedding arrangements. The bride and her mother did it all and dragged Harry along with them. The only time Harry perked up was when he met my brother to discuss the cake. He and Larry became casual friends. But overall

Harry did as he was told until he got drunk. Then he..." She shrugged. "He was aggressive, and I didn't respond well."

Nick reached out, took her hand, and squeezed her fingers. "I'm proud of you, Lexie. You're a woman who won't let people abuse her."

Heat flooded her body and flamed her face. "Harry started crying, and everyone came running. He told his bride and mother that he was taking a leak and I attacked him like a crazed woman."

Mac said, "They believed him?"

"The wedding was called off the next day. I don't really know if they believed him. Probably his bride didn't believe him, or she didn't want to marry a man who urinates in public."

"Underachieving son of a powerful mother who was publicly humiliated. That could very well be your stalker," Tate said. "I'm going to get to work now and track him down. Lexie?"

"What?"

"If it's Harry, how did he get a key to your apartment?"

Nick sat on the arm of Lexie's chair and said, "Didn't you tell me that your brother is selling his condo and Livingston is a real estate agent?"

"Oh." The creepiness skittered down her spine and spread a greasy cold in her stomach. "But Harry's not Larry's real estate agent."

Tate took over. "He'd have a key to the lockbox to your brother's house. He could get in there and find your key. It wouldn't be hard to get it copied and return it before your brother knew it was gone."

"He went to that much trouble?" She tried to understand. "Every time I met with Harry, he just seemed like...Harry. Ruled by the women in his life, and a little pathetic. I tried to be nice to him because I felt sorry for him."

"Delusional stalker," Tate said. "If it's him, he fixated on you because you were nice and he turned it into obsessive love. That kind of delusion will drive the stalker to extremes. I'm going to try and find William Harry Livingston right away. And I'm going to see what my police contacts have on him. In the meantime, Lexie, you be very careful." Tate hung up.

Mac said, "Why don't we pick Shelly up and the four of us get some dinner? I know Shelly wants to talk to you about taking the job here in San Diego. She'd love to have you close by."

Nick stood from the arm of her chair. "Sorry, we have plans."

She looked up at him. "We do? What?"

He looked down at her. "I'm taking you to dinner. Just us."

He was? "Oh." He didn't want Shelly talking her into the job. "Nick, I'm not taking the job. Shelly won't—"

He tugged her to her feet and put his arm around her shoulders. "I want to take you to dinner and spend some time with you."

"Nick's at the Beach?"

Nick watched her look around the two-story

restaurant with its ocean view. "The name is a coincidence, although maybe I should tell you I own the place to impress you. Let's eat downstairs where it's a little quieter. Upstairs is more of a sports bar. But we could play a little pool up there after dinner." He wouldn't mind seeing her lean over a pool table in that short denim skirt. What color panties did she have on? Maybe green ones to match the halter top she wore? He put a stop to his thoughts before he ended up sporting a massive hard-on.

The waitress asked if they wanted to start off with drinks. Lexie ordered a Coke.

He reached out and took her hand. "They have a really good wine list here."

"I'm not a big drinker."

He never thought she was. "Have some wine." He had ruined her fun the other night at Mac and Shelly's, then yesterday when she was surfing. The last thing Lexie needed was anyone else judging her. He knew how much she wanted to break free of the bonds on her. She could do that with him and be safe. He smiled to encourage her.

"Okay, then I'll have Chardonnay."

Nick ordered the same, although he would limit himself to one glass. He was uneasy with the stalker situation and wanted to keep his reflexes sharp. He wore his gun in a shoulder holster under a lightweight jacket. Shredded panties with a death threat was the sign of a really pissed off, delusional stalker. But he didn't want to talk about that tonight. He wanted this evening to be about Lexie.

Keeping hold of her hand, he said, "I wanted to talk to you about the job offer. If you're interested, I think you should—"

She slid her hand from his and fiddled with the silverware. "I'm not going to take it. I have to settle my life first before I think about a new job. I still have the court date Friday, and no matter how nice a deal my lawyer has negotiated, I will have some obligations. And I doubt that Mac mentioned that I've been accused of assault and battery. That's not going to look good on my record. Besides—"

The waitress came, set down their drinks, and they ordered dinner. Lexie chose the artichoke pasta while he had the tortilla-crusted mahimahi.

It struck Nick that she'd been thinking about that job a lot. Did it mean that much to her? After tasting his wine, he said, "Finish your thought. Besides what?"

Setting her wineglass down, she squared her shoulders. "I may fight the charges."

He leaned back in surprise. She didn't look away, but he caught the way she compressed her mouth, probably thinking he didn't agree with her decision. He reached across the table, took the fork she was turning over and over from her hand, and wrapped his fingers around hers. "Good. I hope you do. You can win, Lexie. There's probably someone else who saw William Harry Livingston expose himself."

"I'm sure there is. I don't know why I didn't think of it before." She looked away. "This is a nice place. One of your favorites?"

"I come here sometimes when I'm home. The food is good, the bar upstairs is fun, and I shoot a mean game of pool."

She surprised him by turning her hand over and rubbing her thumb over his wrist and palm. "I guess I really don't know much about you. You like pool." She lifted her gaze from his hand and added, "Do you miss karate? You must have been good."

Shit, her touch was stirring his desire to sizzling. But he didn't want to hurt her feelings by stopping her from touching him. He tried to concentrate on her question. "I'm still good, sweetheart. I'm damned good. I train whenever I can at a nearby studio."

She grinned. "Modest too." Her face sobered. "You must love it, karate, I mean. I thought you left it all behind. Became a bounty hunter to avenge Ellen, I guess."

He couldn't even think about Ellen when Lexie's feathery touch was traveling through him, heating his blood and sending it all to his dick. He just shrugged as an answer.

Lexie's face stiffened slightly. "Sorry, I didn't mean to pry. We'll talk about something else. When do you want to leave for Santa Barbara? I guess we have to leave tomorrow so I'll be there for my court date Friday morning. You need to get back to work. I've wondered how you can just take a whole week off, but, well, never mind. You can be back home by the end of the day."

The waitress arrived and Lexie stopped rambling. While the waitress arranged the food,

Nick's chest tightened and cut off his breath in a rare sensation of panic. As soon as their server left, he blurted out, "I don't want to take you back."

"I have to go back," she answered softly. "We both know that."

That wasn't making him feel any better. He knew damn well they'd end up in bed later, and he'd have her for the whole night, so what was eating at him? Making him feel like he losing something vital to his soul? Whatever it was, it was his problem. He'd taken her out to spend time with her, not to brood. "How's your dinner?"

"It's great. Yours?"

"Good." The forced cheer in her voice irritated him. But he was the one talking about trivial things. She'd asked him about himself and he'd skirted the question. Yet Lexie had trusted him with the details of her life. She'd trusted him with her body, had made love with him in a way that he doubted she'd ever done before. But the thing that made his chest ache was her book. Her dream. Lexie had copied her book and handed it to him to read.

He knew what that book meant to her. She'd shared her cherished dream with him, and that was more intimate and touching than anything anyone else had ever given him.

He wanted to give her a part of himself that had the same meaning, to show her that she was more than a one night stand or vacation sex to him. As they ate, he told her about himself. "I became a bounty hunter because I could go after the bad guys without becoming involved with the victims. I loved

Ellen and yet I couldn't save her. I didn't ever want to feel that again. And the fact that I was alive and she was dead really pissed me off."

"So you paid for living by catching other skips like her ex-husband? A penance?"

He'd never thought of it quite like that. "That's as good a description as any."

"And now?"

He hesitated, but it was time to let go of the past and move forward. "Now I'm tired of being on the road and dealing with scum. No matter how many I capture, more are out there." He'd been thinking about it for a year. Mac and his sister were the only other two people who knew—until now. Too much. He was sharing too much and opening old wounds. Or maybe it was even bigger than that—he was letting Lexie in too close, giving her the power to hurt him. How could he bear to care so much again?

Instinctively, he changed the subject to give himself a moment to regroup. "Would you like dessert?"

She looked up at him with her big brown eyes. "What are you offering?"

Nick's dick twitched. "Stop that. I have to be able to get up and walk out of here."

Her smile was wicked. Teasing.

He leaned forward, surprising himself by asking, "What are you thinking?"

"That we should enjoy the time we have left. In bed." Her grin widened. "And you don't have to feed me to get me there."

He wanted her, God he did. But he hadn't taken her out just to get her in bed. He'd wanted to spend time with her and get to know her better. Maybe he wanted to mean something to her. He'd never been like this, wondering what the woman thought about him. She was so undemanding, it was starting to make him cranky. "There are other things to life than just sex." Oh shit, had he really said that?

She leaned back, her smile slipping. "Okay. If you want dessert, go ahead. I'm not very hungry."

Of course she wasn't. Her life was a fucking nightmare and he was making it worse. She was scared. He'd felt her fear rising since the conversation with Tate. Hell, Lexie had known all along her stalker was dangerous. Thank God she was smart enough to hire a private investigator and get out of Santa Barbara. "I didn't mean that the way it sounded, sweetheart. Please believe me. Just looking at you makes me hard. I just don't want you to think I'm using you for sex." *Huh?* When had the rules changed?

Her smile was strained. "But you are, Nick. And I'm using you. Keep it simple." She broke eye contact and drained her glass of wine.

He paid for dinner, then pulled Lexie to her feet, looking into her eyes. The truth was slowly dawning on him—he couldn't hold anything back from her. No part of himself. This woman had gotten under his skin; she made him hope again. She made him want it all. But if he wanted her trust for more than sex, he had to share the part of himself he'd buried with Ellen. "I want to show you something."

"What?"

He tugged her closer to him just to feel her body against his, uncaring of the people watching them in the restaurant. "A place that's important to me."

"Really?"

His certainty grew with each passing second. Lexie had shown him her book; he wanted to show her this. "Really." He caught her hand and walked out with her.

Nick laughed at her endless questions as he drove through the streets. He'd sparked her curiosity, and she liked a puzzle.

"Can't be landscape because it's dark. It's not your house or apartment—"

That caught him. "How do you know that?"

She laughed. "You keep your private life out of your work. Very wise, of course, considering the dangerous felons you chase, like me. A bar maybe? Or pool hall?" She bit her lip. "But we were just at a restaurant with a bar and pool tables."

He'd never even thought of taking her to his house. It was practically empty anyway, since he was rarely there. He wondered if she'd realize he was showing her more of himself where he was taking her.

She turned in the car seat. "I know! Dancing!"

Damn, he hadn't thought of that either. After their conversation on the beach about going dancing, he should have at least asked her. "Do you want to go dancing? We can go after we stop here." He turned into the parking lot of a strip mall.

"We're here?" She leaned forward against the

seat belt, taking in the flower shop, small bookstore, postal annex, health food store, and upscale coffeehouse. There was an empty building between the bookstore and coffeehouse. "This is what you want to show me?"

Instinctively, he knew she'd understand. "Trust me."

She nodded. After undoing her seat belt, she opened the door and swung her bare legs out.

Nick watched her ass as she stood up. Then he grabbed his keys and got out. He led her to the door of the empty suite, found the right key and opened the door. He reached in and turned on the light. "Come on in."

Lexie walked in ahead of him.

He let the door shut and looked around. They were in the main part of the studio. Right now all that was in there were a couple of long folding tables covered in plans they were working on and some folding chairs. The studio would open in two months.

Lexie walked in a circle, taking in the space. Then she went through a hallway that led to a second room for smaller classes. She headed back into the hall and found the closet, a bathroom, and the last room at the end of the hallway.

Nick followed her, turning on lights as he went. In his head, he could hear the grunts, the kicks, the sound of flesh hitting boards to break them. He could smell the sweat, almost feel the adrenaline. He could see the faces of the students as they mastered tough techniques, or see the droop of posture when they couldn't get it.

She stopped in the very back room, which shared a wall with the coffeehouse. "You've already decided to give up bounty hunting. That's why you had time to hang out all week at the resort."

She looked so pretty standing there, the lights catching the shimmering sun streaks in her brown hair, set off by the green top. Her shoulders were golden tan, her face open and interested.

"Yeah, I've decided. I'm signing papers with Mac. This will be our karate studio."

A muffled bang and scattered noises bounced in the empty room, making Lexie jump. A burst of giggles bled through the wall, and she laughed at herself. "That's from the coffeehouse next door? I wonder if all the noise in here will bother them."

Noting her jumpiness, he stroked her arm. "No, this room will be the office. And we're going to add some soundproofing to the walls of the two studio rooms."

She smiled. "You've thought a lot about this. And you have experience since you and Mac had a studio before." She headed out the door to the main area and stopped at the two tables shoved together. She set her tiny purse down and pushed aside a plastic box stuffed with office supplies to look at the plans. After a couple of minutes, she looked over her left shoulder at him. "Thanks, Nick."

He could barely breathe. "What for?"

Her smile glowed. "For sharing this with me. When you talked about karate at dinner, I could tell you loved it."

Oh hell. He latched onto her shoulders, turned

her to draw her to him. Right now, Lexie seemed more important than karate. Or anything. Hell. To stop from thinking about that, he kissed her.

He wasn't going to be able to walk away this time.

Chapter 9

LEXIE WRAPPED HER ARMS AROUND Nick, feeling the hard length of his body pressed up against hers. He'd given her a piece of himself by showing her the building that held his dreams. He made her feel special.

Right now, he was making her feel desired. A deep longing welled up in her. She wanted Nick, needed him. Pressing one hand to the back of his head, she slid her tongue into his mouth.

He groaned against her, stroking his tongue along hers. He sank both his hands into her hair, tugging her head back. "Lexie."

Every time he said her name in that growl, she nearly came. Her breath hitched and picked up speed.

"You aren't a job," Nick said. "You've never been a job. And you sure as hell aren't just sex."

Oh God, she couldn't lie to him. Not like this. "It's okay, Nick. We both agreed—"

"I'm changing the agreement. I can't let you go. I

can't walk away from you. I didn't ever want to feel this much again. Then I met you, and I lost control. Nothing I did helped. Even after we made love, I just wanted you more."

Her body melted into him against her will. But panic gnawed at her stomach. "Nick, maybe it's just the circumstances reminding you of Ellen." She couldn't compete with a ghost, didn't want to.

His mouth curved up. "You're nothing like her, Lexie. Nothing. You have a deep wild streak that she never had. I needed to protect her from the world. With you, it's different. I only need to stand by your side, be a team. All the responsibility doesn't fall on me." He kissed her, then added, "You gave me your book to read. You poured such power and passion into that book, and you trusted me with it."

He understood what her writing meant to her. It was more than trust, it was respect. He respected her dream, just like he'd respected her decision not to sleep with him four months ago. When he had kissed her, she'd melted into him, wanted him. But he'd sent her home, respecting that she didn't do one-night stands.

But with Nick, it wasn't a one-night stand, it was making love with a man who knew and accepted her. He'd stirred in her a wild passion that she'd fought to contain her whole life. Nick wouldn't allow her to hold back. That was what he wanted from her, the real her. She didn't regret giving it to him. She would give it to him until they parted. But they both had to be realistic. "Nick, I have to go back. Your life is here."

He dropped his hands from her hair. "Don't move." He walked across the room and locked the door. Then he returned to her. "Don't stop trusting me, Lexie. Not now. We've got something special. Trust me enough for us to see where this thing between us goes." He slid off his jacket, unhooked the shoulder harness with his gun, and laid them on the ground. Then he took off his shirt.

"What are you doing?" He had her off balance, scared to death, then she looked at his broad shoulders and his powerful chest and she didn't feel quite so frightened. He looked big enough, strong enough to lean on just a little bit. And he looked yummy enough to lick...

"I'm going to make love to you and show you what I feel for you. I didn't bring a condom, so we'll save that for later." He took his shoes off and stripped out of his jeans.

Right down to his navy blue boxers with his erection pressing against the soft material. His thighs were corded and tight with tension. Sexual tension. She lifted her gaze.

Raw hunger sizzled in his eyes.

Swallowing her emotion, she said, "I do. I took a couple from your box." What would he think of her? She reached into her purse and pulled out a condom.

Taking it from her fingers, he leaned in to her. "You're not a good girl anymore, are you, Lexie?"

He was close enough to her that they could share skin, overwhelming her. "No."

Setting the condom on the table, he added, "You

want to be bad, don't you? Not worry that someone will be mad? Withhold their affection because you didn't do it their way."

God, he knew her. She swallowed the feeling building in her throat. "Yes." Her voice sounded desperate, but she trusted him. He excited her, yet she felt safe. That's what he was telling her, that she could trust him to accept her for herself. She moved a step back, her butt hitting the table. Reaching behind her, she untied the bottom ends of her halter top and pulled it over her head.

Nick's gaze heated and his fingers curled into his palms. His dick pulsed hard against his boxers.

The power she had over him was intoxicating. After dropping her top, she undid the zipper of her skirt and let it fall. She kicked it off, followed by her shoes.

His voice was low and rough. "Light green panties. So pale I can see through them."

She reached out, snagged the waistband of his boxers, and slid them down to his thighs. His cock sprang out, thick and long. She wrapped her fingers around him, feeling the silky hot skin of his rigid erection. It twitched with excitement in her hand. When she saw Nick reach for her, she dropped to her knees and said, "I get to do what I want." Then she did, sliding her tongue over him until he leaned forward, slapping his hands on the table to steady himself.

Then she sucked him in deep.

"I'm at your mercy." He panted the words. His whole body shuddered. "Watching my cock slide in and out of your mouth is making me break out in a sweat."

She slid her tongue over the sensitive head and hummed.

"Jesus." He barely breathed the word, his body jerking.

She cupped his balls and they drew up tight. Smiling, she slid him from her mouth, looked up, and teased, "Are you complaining?"

His chest heaved and his hair fell over his face. The muscles and tendons all stood out on his arms when he braced himself on the table. "Are you enjoying tormenting me, Lexie?"

Like she had to think about that. "Yes."

His grin had a pained edge to it. "Good." He pushed off the table, reached down, and pulled her to her feet. After sliding her panties down, he grasped her waist and lifted her onto the table. Putting his hands on her knees, he spread her legs and looked down at her, then back at her face. "You're so wet, and I haven't touched you yet."

She loved the hard, sensual shape of his face. She loved the way he made her feel safe and wild at the same time. "I touched you."

His gaze flared hot. Picking up the condom, he ripped it open and sheathed himself.

He leaned down, capturing a nipple and pulling it deep in his mouth.

Her thighs clenched as he fired a deep ache in her.

He stepped between her legs, keeping her thighs spread, and slid a finger along her folds, finding her swollen clit. Shifting, he sucked her other nipple and rubbed her clit.

She writhed, grabbing his shoulders for support.

Nick lifted his head, his eyes fierce. Wrapping his arms around her, he said, "Lie back on the table."

She trusted him, letting him lay her on the two tables pushed together.

Leaning over her, he opened his mouth in a hot and hungry kiss. Consuming her. She opened beneath him, not holding anything back.

When he released her mouth and stood up, she felt a wave of cool air replace the heat of his body.

His gaze never left hers. He picked up her legs. "Brace your thighs against me."

She felt the heat of his stomach and chest press against the backs of her thighs. It was an awkward position...unless she trusted him to support her. And he did, reaching down to lift her hips up. With her legs against his chest, she was wide open to him. He kept her gaze as he slid inside her, slow and sure. Once he was buried in her, he started stroking in and out. "I can feel every inch of you taking me in. Feel the spot that gives you so much pleasure."

She gasped, her nerves feeling singed and raw. "How do you do that?" She didn't know. No one had reached so deeply inside her.

Holding her hips, he thrust again. "You're so damned responsive to me, all I have to do is follow your body." He looked down, watching as he thrust again. Then he closed his eyes on a groan. "You're swallowing me."

The cords on his neck stood out, his mouth was drawn tight, his whole body rigid as he kept his rhythm slow and wicked. She knew he was holding back, trying to give her as much pleasure as possible. "Nick, I want all of you."

His gaze snapped open. "Just trying to let you catch up." He drove himself in, lifting her hips to take him.

He filled her up, touching and teasing a spot inside her that made her squirm and beg. "More!"

He let go then, his fingers digging into her hips as he shoved himself into her, over and over. Harder, deeper, the craving coiling so deep inside her, she bit her lip. "Nick..." He had her at his mercy, driving her higher and higher until the pressure released, her orgasm ripping through her. Her body opened wider as Nick drove in, arched his powerful body, and came in violent shudders.

He lowered her hips and slid her legs down. Bending over her, he brushed the hair off her face and said, "I think you might have killed me."

She laughed, her body so boneless and fluid it was hard to tell where she ended and he began. She opened her mouth—

But another voice intruded. "She didn't kill you, but I will."

The threatening voice behind Nick made the hairs on the back of his neck stand straight up.

Guilt shoved hard at him. How the hell did someone else get inside? That noise earlier, the one he'd laughed off as coming from the coffee shop. Damnit, the bastard must had slipped inside and hidden when he and Lexie had been in the back office. He should have checked, should have been more careful.

Instead, he was bare-assed and buried inside Lexie. He screwed up. Again. The only thing he cared about now was protecting her.

He pulled out and whirled around, shoving Lexie hard to knock her off the end of the table. "Under the table," he ordered her.

He heard the thump of her falling to the ground, along with the crash of the box of office supplies, but his attention was on the man holding the gun. He stood about five foot eight inches, and was in his late twenties, with thinning brown hair. His face was red with anger. The vein in his temple throbbed. He glared at Nick with jealous hatred.

Nick didn't recognize him, but it had to be Lexie's stalker.

"Harry! What are you doing?"

Nick's heart stopped when Lexie rose up beside him, clutching his T-shirt to her body as a shield. "Get down," he snarled at her, while reaching to his thighs to yank up his boxers.

Livingston's face got redder. "Whore. I told you to wait for me!" He waved the gun at Lexie.

A possessive rage exploded in Nick like nothing he'd ever felt. The sight of the gun moving toward Lexie made everything crystal clear.

He loved her and would kill to keep her safe.

He would die to let her live.

He sized up their chances. None of them were good. His gun was on the floor on the other side of Lexie. He tried distraction first. "Let Lexie go. You don't want to hurt her. I forced her." Delusional stalkers tended to build a story line in their heads—Nick tried to feed it.

The man bared his teeth. "I saw what that whore did to you. She liked it!" He turned his attention to her. "Bitch whore, I told you, you'll die!"

He saw the second Livingston tightened his finger on the trigger. Oh fuck, he was going to shoot Lexie. Nick couldn't reach the man in time to time to stop him. He only had one choice. Pivoting, he threw himself on Lexie.

A gunshot exploded, the noise reverberating like a bomb.

As Nick hit the ground, a searing pain dug into his left thigh, but his years of training helped him roll to keep Lexie from absorbing all his weight. As soon as he felt his back hit the floor, he tried to roll over again to get Lexie beneath him.

She shoved him off her.

His thigh screamed, a hot flash of sheer agony that ripped through every nerve in his body. Sweat slicked his body. "Christ."

Too late, he realized Lexie was on her knees next to him. She yelled, "You shot him!" and brought her hand back in an overhand pitch and threw something.

A wet smack and distinctive crunch sounded.

"Ow! You..." The words trailed off, followed by a thump.

Nick rolled over, snagged the shoulder harness, and got his gun out. He used the table to pull himself to his feet.

Livingston was sprawled face first on the ground, with a gun and a plain old stapler lying next to him. Stunned, Nick said, "You hit him with a stapler?"

Lexie yanked on her panties, then ran over, scooped up the gun, and put it on the table. "He shot you. I can't believe he shot you!" She grabbed a chair and put it behind him. "Sit."

Nick did what she told him, still in shock. "You knocked him out with a stapler. Mac isn't going to believe this."

After yanking on her clothes, she knelt in front of Nick, with his shirt in her hand and a cell phone pressed against her ear as she called nine-one-one. She pressed the shirt to his thigh.

He hissed and focused on Lexie's bent head, the shimmering colors in her brown hair. He forced himself to breathe and control the pain.

She hung up the phone and looked up at him. "I'm so sorry."

The pain didn't matter anymore. Taking hold of her face with his free hand, he said, "You saved our lives with a stapler. What the hell are you sorry for?" He wasn't sure he could have gotten to his gun fast enough.

"I didn't want you hurt because of me. You knew he meant to shoot me and—" She shuddered.

He ran his hand over her clenched jaw, into her hair, and pulled her head to rest against his stomach. "I love you, Lexie. No way was I letting that prick shoot you. He's hurt you enough."

She lifted her head to look up at him. "I was terrified when he shot you and then rage took over. I couldn't let him kill you or hurt... You love me?"

Nick checked to make sure Livingston was still passed out, keeping his gun in his grip just in case. But he focused on his woman. He wasn't afraid of love anymore; there was no room for fear with Lexie. She was too alive, too vital, and too goddamned courageous. He had to be as strong and fearless as she was. She made him willing to risk anything, even his heart, to hold her. He leaned down and said, "You love me too, Lexie. You don't ever have to be afraid to love me or be loved by me. You're everything I want in a lover." He brushed his mouth over hers just as they heard the sirens of the police cars roaring into the parking lot.

Four months later

She sat on the cold bench, watching the waterfall in the colored lights. The nights were cool, and she shivered. The little park was empty now. This afternoon it had been filled with people celebrating a family reunion. Lexie had arranged it as the event coordinator. She loved her job. She loved her life. She had a small apartment, she dated Nick, and she had friends. Her book was done, and while she was waiting to hear from publishers, she had started another one. She felt whole and happy.

William Harry Livingston had been arrested, and the charges against her were dropped. She'd only gone back to her apartment in Santa Barbara to make arrangements to store her furniture. Not long after that, she had moved to San Diego and taken the job at Sand Castle Resort. Nick and Mac had outfitted her apartment with an excellent security system, but most nights she slept with Nick by her side. No man, no person, had ever made Lexie feel strong and self-confident, and yet safe, like Nick did.

She shivered again in the cool spray from the waterfall. Her parents were still trying to get her to return to Santa Barbara, but they no longer tried guilt. They were horrified to realize she had been in serious danger and they hadn't believed her.

Her mom had finally insisted that Larry and Amber grow up and stop leeching off her. Her dad had admitted to Lexie that he was terrified of losing her mom after the heart attack. He cried, and Lexie began to realize that she hadn't been the best daughter either. She should have realized the trauma her parents were going through.

"Lexie." Nick strode up and stopped in front of her.

Her heart tripped, the same as it always did when he called her name. She didn't know why he wanted to meet her here tonight, but he knew how much she loved the little resort park. "Is your class over already?" She'd watched him many times when he worked out, sparred, or taught. She was always stunned at the power and grace in his moves.

"Yep." He reached down and pulled her into his arms. "You're cold."

She pressed her face into his T-shirt. "Not anymore. Hmm, you smell good." He must've showered at the studio after his class.

He put his hand on the back of her head. "You love it here by this fountain, don't you?"

She looked up at him. "Yes. It's where I found myself that night, then I found you."

He smiled. "Come here." He dropped his hand, pulling her closer to the fountain.

She laughed, hanging back. "The water's cold!"

Nick turned to face her. "That night, when I went after you and saw you standing in the water, I knew then. I was in love with you. And each day, I love you more."

Her heart melted. "I love you too."

He reached into the pocket of his pants and pulled out a small box.

Her heart stuttered.

Nick opened the box and took out a ring. It sparkled in the moonlight and caught all the colors of the footlights. He reached for her left hand. "Marry me, Lexie."

She stared at him sliding the ring on her finger.

"Here, in the place where we found each other. I don't care if you want a big wedding or a small one. Please marry me."

She lifted her gaze to his face. "Oh, Nick. I love

you. Yes, I'll marry you. But can it be small? Just us, your mom, sister and her husband, and my family?"

He frowned. "Including your asshole brother?"

"Yes, including him."

He pulled her close into his arms. "Anything for you." He kissed her long and slow, his hands skimming beneath her shirt to brand her back.

Fiery heat bloomed between them. Her nipples throbbed and her belly tightened with need. Lexie pulled back to get her breath. "You always do this to me."

"Do what?"

"Make me want you with just a kiss."

His mouth curved into a wickedly arrogant grin. "I was a confirmed bachelor until you came along and rocked my world with that first kiss. But tell me, Miss Wedding Planner—"

She didn't bother correcting him with her current title of Event Coordinator since she still planned a few weddings. "What?"

He arched an eyebrow. "Aren't you wondering why I didn't get down on my knees to pop the question?"

Nope. His proposal was perfect, beautiful and real like the man himself. But she'd play along. "Because you didn't want to be cliché?"

Nick sank his hand into her silky hair, tilting her head up to stare into her eyes. "Because I'm going to get down on my knees for something else." He walked her back toward the fountain. "I'm going to kiss you until you come. Just like that night, only this time you'll have my ring on your finger and my heart in your hands."

"Nick!" A rush of love, lust and laughter swarmed over her, drenching her in happiness. "It's cold and someone might see us!"

He scooped her up into his arms and carried her out of the little park. "Then we'll go to the room I reserved for us. But I'm going to have you. Tonight and always."

She framed his face in her palms and smiled. "You already do."

~The End~

Coming March 20, 2017

The Sex on the Beach Book Club

by JENNIFER LYON

WRITING AS JENNIFER APODACA

Originally published by Kensington Publishing Corp. in 2007

Turn the page to read an excerpt!

Chapter 7

Holly Hillbay was the best damned private investigator in Goleta, California, but you couldn't tell it from the week she was having. Losing her bread-and-butter client, whom she did routine new-hire background checks for, was bad enough. But she knew Brad the Cad, her ex-fiancé, had something to do with that, which made her furious.

She channeled her frustration into her new case—going undercover in a book club. That was what brought her to the Books on the Beach bookstore on a Tuesday evening. Pausing outside the door, she inhaled a breath of the damp, salty air from the nearby ocean. The preppy, probably over-educated bookstore owner Wes Brockman, and the very married Tanya Shaker, were about to have their sordid little affair exposed like a celebrity biography.

That thought cheered her up and she went inside. The ringing bell over the door still echoed as she quickly scanned the bookstore. The first thing she saw was an inviting sitting area done in white wicker with ocean blue cushions. That was bookended by a checkout counter with a coffee and beverage station next to it on her right, and a wall-sized bookcase featuring new releases directly across from the door. Beyond the sitting area were rows of dark bookcases. The whole atmosphere exuded sophisticated comfort where readers could leisurely browse until they selected the books they wanted to buy.

A deep voice from behind her asked, "Can I help you?"

Holly turned around and felt a slap of lust that could have been right out of a romance novel. Since she wasn't a big romance reader, she was going to have to blame it on the man—he was hot. Sun-streaked brown hair and vivid green eyes set in a face that had a little George Clooney going on. His mouth was full and oozed sensual promises. His jaw wore just enough of a shadow to make her want to run her hand along his cheek to feel the texture.

Oh yeah, he could help her end her long dry spell in the bedroom. She blinked and reminded her deprived hormones that she was on the job. *Damn it.* "Hi, I'm Holly. I'm here for the book club." She hoped her week had taken a turn for the better, and this guy turned out to be anyone but Wes Brockman.

He smiled, crinkling the skin around his green eyes. "I'm Wes. Book club is just getting started." He held a hand up toward a door that opened on the left side of the store.

It figured. She revised her opinion of the bookstore owner: *Sexy as hell, preppy and probably over-educated. Oh, and he screwed married women, probably because he could.* Her hormone levels banked down to a mere sizzle. Managing to look past her lust, she saw his expensive clothes mixed with the self-confidence that came with money and success. Holly immediately pegged the bookstore as his hobby and not the career that made him rich and sophisticated.

Tearing her gaze from him, she turned and headed toward the room he indicated. It was about the size of the master bedroom in her condo, and had four long tables set in a rectangle shape. She estimated about eighteen people gathered around it. Thermoses of coffee and plates of cookies were set out on the tables. A brief look around showed her a door that led to a small bathroom and another door that was closed— probably a storage area or office. There were poster-sized book covers on the walls, adding color and energy to the room.

She scanned the more than a dozen women and three men, and spotted Tanya Shaker. She looked just like the picture Holly had of her, shoulder-length blond hair, lots of makeup, and an industrial-strength bra that pushed her breasts up to her chin in her low-cut black T-shirt. She sat with a lifeguard-handsome man on her right and an empty chair on her left.

Perfect.

"Holly, take a seat anywhere," Wes's hand brushed her arm then was gone.

A warm shiver rolled down her spine, catching her off guard. *Must be a full moon or something.* Clearly her libido had not gotten the message that Wes was a player. She didn't date rich men who indiscriminately screwed women. In fact, she didn't date much at all these days. Men were a troublesome distraction from her career.

Pulling her thoughts back to the job, she walked over to Tanya and slid into the seat next to her. "Hi, I'm Holly. Have you belonged to the book club long?" In Holly's experience, women talked more than men—usually because they mixed up sex and love.

Tanya did the girl-to-girl scan and said, "About a month."

Holly got to work. "I just heard about the book club. Thought I'd give it a try. Only three men, huh?" There was Wes Brockman at the end of the tables on her right. A guy sitting next to him who was a little older, darker, wearing blue-tinted glasses that didn't mask the deep suspicion in his dark eyes. Then there was the man on the other side of Tanya, who leaned forward and looked at Holly.

"I'm Cullen. Would you like to use my book?" He pushed the book toward her. "I'm sure Tanya will let me share with her."

Holly took the book and glanced at the title. *"Wicked" Women Whodunit.*

Tanya grinned at her. "It's good. I read it and I'm not much of a reader."

Holly swallowed the urge to ask what the hell

she was doing at a book club if she didn't read. But she knew why Tanya was there. What really surprised her was how careful Tanya was being. Women usually gave it away long before the men did. Especially the player types like Wes Brockman. They were used to woman after woman moving through their beds and seldom gave them a thought outside of the sheets. "Yeah, I read it. Love those women who go after what they want." She *had* actually read the book.

Tanya turned to look the other way. "Me, too."

Holly presumed Tanya was looking down the table at Wes. *A secret lover's look?*

"Holly," Wes said from his end of the table. "Did I hear you say you read this book?"

She felt it again—that zing as his gaze met hers. What kind of crap was that? It was like a drippy movie moment and she refused to acknowledge it. She focused on her answer instead. "Yes, I did. I guess I'm surprised that your book club picked a book like this."

He arched his eyebrows. "Like what?"

She knew a challenge when she heard one. This was more comfortable territory for her. "This blatantly sexy. The heroines in this book get caught up in a mystery and are aggressive about solving it. And they aren't shy about sleeping with the man they choose."

Cullen, sitting on the other side of Tanya, said, "My kind of woman."

Wes cut his gaze from Holly to him. "Why is that, Cullen?"

Cullen flashed a boyish grin. "I don't see why men should always have to chase women. I don't mind being chased. Or caught."

Laughter rolled down both sides of the table.

Except, Holly noticed, for the three women who sat across from her. They looked at one another, all three of them wearing tight-lipped expressions. She could almost feel their collective reaction to Cullen. What was that about? What had Cullen done to annoy or embarrass those three?

One of the women spoke up. "The stories in this anthology are not just about sex. They're about a relationship developing when a man and woman are thrown together in mysterious circumstances."

"Very well stated, Nora," Wes said.

Holly studied Nora, seeing a woman who had home-dyed brown hair, brown eyes, and a gentle manner. Maybe she'd been a romantic when she was younger and still believed just a little bit.

The woman next to Nora said, "The men just want sex."

"That's a little harsh, Maggie," Wes answered.

Maggie wore a tailored suit and constantly checked her cell phone. She glared at Cullen before she dropped her gaze back to her phone.

All kinds of undercurrents were going on in this book club, the kind that usually had to do with sex. Was this a book club or a sex club? The women all seemed pretty easygoing with Wes. It was Cullen who was causing reactions.

And guess who was sitting next to Cullen? Had Holly's client, Tanya's husband Phil, been wrong about who Tanya was doing the sheet tango with?

Just as an awkward silence was ready to engulf the room, Wes tossed out another question. "Does murder break down social expectations and up the stakes so that the characters are more likely to come together sexually?"

The man was smooth. Holly snorted and looked up at Wes.

He cocked an eyebrow. "Did you say something. Holly?"

What did she care? She was here to do a job and once it was done, she would never see these people again. So she told the truth. "That's crap. It's lust, pure and simple. Lust has been around for centuries. Women feel lust, too."

"Oh yeah," Tanya whispered in a low sexy voice, and leaned, boobs first, into Cullen on the other side of her.

Oh yeah, *Holly thought*, Phil suspected the wrong man of sleeping with his wife.

Wes recaptured her attention when he asked, "What about love? Traditionally, women have searched for love."

She couldn't look away from him. Everyone had turned to watch her, but she couldn't care enough to break the connection between her and Wes. There was something deep and mysterious about him, and it called to all Holly's instincts to solve the puzzle. What brought a man like Wes to owning a bookstore in a beach town? His question tugged at her old wounds, but she lifted her chin and told him her truth, a truth she learned the hard way. "I prefer lust over love. Lust is simple and straightforward."

Wes had no idea how he'd gotten through the remainder of the book club. Holly's *lust over love* comment had burrowed into his brain and taken up residence in his sex drive. There was something incredibly sexy about the newest member of his book club.

Watching Holly as she got up from the table, he thought she looked a little like the character Lilly Rush, from the *Cold Case* TV show. She had her hair tucked up in that same casual-messy style, though it was a darker blonde. Since he'd had the pleasure of walking up behind her, he got an eye full of her long lean figure and her mouthwatering ass. But when she'd turned around, it had been her blue eyes that captured his attention. Gray-blue, the color was hard to define—a bit of clear blue sky mixed with the churning waters of a stormy ocean.

Oh yeah, she'd caught his interest. She'd made him feel *something* when he hadn't felt *anything* in a hell of a long time.

So yeah, she was sexy, he was interested—but he was also wary, more from habit than anything. Holly seemed to have more interest in the people of the club than the book. He hadn't seen her in the bookstore before and no one else in the room seemed to recognize her. So how had she found out about the book club? Or had being in hiding for three years just made him paranoid?

Gazing around the room, he saw that Helene Essex had cornered Cullen, while Tanya looked daggers at them. That torrid situation was going to explode soon; he just hoped it didn't happen in his bookstore. He didn't need the attention and headaches it would bring.

Cullen was the kind of man Wes despised. He used and discarded women, notching his belt as he went along. Wes had nothing against honest sex for the sake of sex alone. Over the last few years, it had been the only sex he had. But he never lied to the women about his feelings or let them believe he was interested in a long term relationship. Tearing his gaze from Cullen, he looked for the woman who was occupying his thoughts.

He spotted Holly holding a copy of *"Wicked" Women Whodunit* and talking to a couple of women, then she broke away. He intercepted her. "Hey," he said, watching as she turned to him, settling her smoke-blue gaze on him. His gut clenched with a thread of desire. He really liked her eyes, and the way she looked right at him. But he didn't know if that was real or a phony sincerity. Wes had spent years ferreting out exactly what people's intentions were. Surely he could handle one young woman. He pulled out his most charming smile. "So how did you find out about our book club?"

"Word of mouth." She grinned. "But this isn't what I expected from a book club."

"No?" Leaving his answer open-ended to see how she'd reply, he noted her vague answer and change of subject. His interest kept ramping up, but the instincts that kept him at the top of his game in his old job told him that Holly was interested in more than just his book club. She was almost too alert, and she didn't volunteer anything about herself.

She shook her head. "I expected Oprah books."

"Ah. The realistic, and predominately tragic, endings. I've had enough of those in my life, how about you?" He didn't let his thoughts stray to the tragic endings, or the deadly mistakes he'd made. He lived with the guilt, but he didn't wallow in it.

Her eyes hardened. "Who doesn't?"

She wasn't going to spill her guts in the first minute. Damn, she was a challenge. He decided to try a little flirting. "So you don't like books with tragic endings. But you do like sexy anthologies."

She leaned her hips back against the table. "Fast-paced and sexy are more my style. You?"

Hell, yeah. Looking at her, with her breasts pushing against that tank top, and her intense gaze, he was completely and one hundred percent into fast-paced and sexy. If flirting, companionship, and maybe sex was what she wanted, he was on board and ready. "Fast-paced and sexy work for me. Are you free tonight to get a drink or coffee?"

Her blue eyes shaded to nearly gray. "I would think someone like you would have plans."

Wes narrowed his gaze. What was her game? Her remark had come out more like an accusation. "Nope. No plans once I close up the store." He left the ball in her court.

She smiled, but her gaze roamed around the room then down to her watch. "Can I have a rain check? I have to run. Thank you for an interesting evening."

Ice water chased out the heat in his gut as suspicion climbed up over his sex drive. She was up to something. "You're in a hurry?"

She started moving away. "Afraid so."

Wes followed her to the front of the store to see what she had been watching. As she opened the door and left, he caught sight of Tanya and Cullen walking ahead of her.

What was Holly doing? It appeared to him she was following Cullen and Tanya. Why? Could she be one of Cullen's castoffs? But Cullen hadn't acted as if he knew her. Wes was so intent on watching her walk away, he nearly jumped at the voice behind him.

"Check her out before you get in her pants."

Wes turned to his best friend. These days, George played the retired businessman. He fudged the facts on the business he retired from and other minor details—like his name, rank, and social security number. But then, who was he to complain? George was the one who helped Wes obtain his new name and social security number. "She look dangerous to you?"

"Hell, yes. That woman instantly drained the blood from your head to your dick. That's the kind of shit that can get you killed."

Wes laughed. "I must be getting old if I'm that obvious." He sobered up. "But that woman is up to something. She seemed surprised at what book the club is reading, so why did she want to be in our book club?"

George looked over his glasses at Wes. "Want me to find out?"

Oh no, this one was all his. Wes was going to get to the bottom of sexy Holly. "No, I want you to stay here and watch the store. I'm going to go see just what Ms. Lust Over Love is up to."

Since Wes knew where Cullen and Tanya were going, if Holly really was following them, it shouldn't be hard to catch up to her.

Holly stood on the docks a mile from the bookstore and watched as the boat motored away, carrying Tanya and Cullen under the full moon. No two ways about it, she was screwed. She had done her preliminary research on Tanya Shaker and Wes Brockman.

But she had the wrong guy. Judging by the hand-holding, giggling, and Cullen's hand on Tanya's ass, Tanya was having an extramarital affair with Cullen, not Wes. Her client had been so sure his wife was cheating with the bookstore owner, Wes. "Shit," she muttered to herself.

"Problem?"

Holly jumped as she watched Wes walk out from the shadows between two stores on the other side of the dock. Had he been spying on her? *What the hell?* She glared at him. "What are you doing here? And why are you sneaking up on me?"

He leaned against the wood rail. "Following you, which requires a certain stealth."

She studied Brockman. The evening was cool, the moon was full, and there was a spill of lights from surrounding businesses now that he had emerged from the shadows. He looked dangerous, sexy, and very Bond-like in his expensive clothes and casual demeanor. As if following a woman he just met was perfectly acceptable for a man who owned a bookstore. Not in Holly's world. Who was this guy? "What are you, some kind of stalker?"

His eyes crinkled, but he didn't quite smile. His full lips did a slight, sarcastic curve. "Call me curious. Why did you follow Cullen and Tanya?"

Seriously, what did he care? She tried to control her annoyance enough to fix a sincere smile on her face. "I wanted to return his book." She raised her hand to show him the book Cullen had loaned her, then had forgotten in his hurry to get Tanya out to sea and naked.

Wes dropped his gaze to the book then looked back to her face. He pushed off the rail and took a long step toward her. "Give the book to me. I'll return it to him."

Inhaling, she caught his scent, something very woodsy mixed with male heat. Sensual. A little quiver danced in her stomach. She blinked and made herself focus. Her target wasn't Brockman, it was Cullen, who had just sailed off for an evening of moonlit sex. Experience taught her that the illicit lovers wouldn't be back for a couple of hours. In the meantime, Wes knew Cullen so she could get the information she needed from him. "I'd really like to thank Cullen myself. What's his last name? I'll look him up."

He leaned down and said in a low tone, "And how do I know you're not a stalker with murder on her mind?"

Oh boy, she was getting a bad case of poor judgment. Wes was a little mysterious and a little dark, two qualities that made her very curious. Why would he follow her to the docks? Because she turned down his invitation for drinks? Or another reason? And damn it, did he have to be so powerfully male? Sexy? He had that deep, passionate quality in a man that made a woman think that when she was naked with him, he'd be solely focused on her. Maybe her hormones needed a dip in the ocean. To Wes, she answered, "Why would I be stalking Cullen? I just want to return his book."

Wes moved close enough to touch her, to make her feel like he *might* touch her. But he didn't. "Guess you'll have to find another way." He turned and walked away.

Holly stood there, a little stunned. Was that payback for her turning him down in the bookstore? Shaking it off, she put Wes out of her mind. She could find out Cullen's last name on her own. She went around to a couple of the businesses, and stopped people on the docks, asking questions. But she drew a big fat zero in her quest for information on Cullen.

After twenty minutes. Holly knew she was wasting her time. She needed Cullen's last name to start doing research on him, and for her reports. Her client needed pictures and detailed reports—including Cullen's last name—to prove Tanya was cheating on him. Phil needed those to invoke a clause in the prenuptial agreement that would significantly reduce the amount of money Tanya would get.

She was sure that Wes knew Cullen's last name. All she had to do was convince him to tell her. Holly hurried through the cool night and reached the bookstore just in time to see Wes come outside, turn around, and lock the door.

Slowing her pace, she walked up. "Hi." Damn, he was still sexy in that overbearing male way.

He pulled his key out of the lock, then turned his gaze on her. "Change your mind?" He glanced down at the book in her hand. "Want me to return Cullen's book?" He added a grin that should be labeled as dangerous.

Holly leaned against the side of the bookstore and shrugged. "I have time to kill. Thought I'd see if you still wanted to get a drink. Unless"—she opened her eyes wide—"you really are afraid that I'm a stalker with murder on my mind."

A small smile tugged at his mouth as he shoved his keys into his pants pocket. "If not murder, then what—sex?"

Oh yeah. Wait, no! God, she was weak tonight. Maybe it was her bad week. She decided to change tactics. "I asked you out for a drink, Brockman. All you have to say is that you aren't interested." She started to walk away.

"Does that work?" he called after her.

She'd only gone a couple feet when she pivoted. "What?"

"The offensive. Does it work?"

A grin tugged at her mouth. "Most of the time. But then, I don't usually have to beg men for their company."

He directed his gaze in a slow examination down her body, clad in a burgundy tank top and form-fitting jeans, then back to her face. His green eyes darkened. "Tell me more about this begging."

Down, girl. What was it about him? She shot back, "For that, you'd have to buy the drinks."

He stepped closer, throttling his voice down to a dangerous rumble. "Sex on the Beach?"

She swore the ocean roared in her head. Her hormones surged up into huge waves of longing washing over her. "You're offering me sex on the beach?"

His grin widened, crinkling his gorgeous eyes. "The drink. What did you think I meant?"

Her thighs tightened in response. *Get a grip, Hillbay—it's just a reaction to a handsome man and a long dry spell of no sex.* Holly was all for sex, but on her terms. She always kept her emotions in check. She was the cool one—the one that walked away when the relationship had played out. It was time to take back the power. "That information will cost you more than the price of a drink."

He didn't hesitate. "Name your price."

"Steak." She was hungry. And food might keep her from thinking about sex.

"Done. You can follow me in your car."

She was practically dizzy from the pace he set. Or maybe that was pent-up lust breaking free. "Follow you where?"

"My house on the beach. I'll make the drinks and we'll grill some steaks out on my deck and watch the waves. Or maybe listen to the waves, since it's dark out." His grin suggested more than wave-watching.

She thought about that, but in the end, Wes had what she wanted. Information on Cullen.

Not sex.

She lifted her chin. "I'll follow you. I can spare an hour or so."

He nodded like it was no more than he expected.

Annoyed, she said, "I'm not sleeping with you."

He moved up to her until she felt the brush of his breath. "No?"

A tremor in her belly spread wet heat. *Keep control of the situation.* "I don't go to bed on the first date."

He reached down and picked up her free hand in his larger one. "Kiss on the first date?"

She should put a stop to this, but the feel of his hand wrapped around hers was warm and sensual. She opened her mouth to tell him they weren't dating, but ended up saying, "If I like the man."

He ran his thumb over her palm. "You like me. Make out?"

Regaining her wits, she jerked her hand away. "Ain't gonna happen, book boy."

His face blanked at the nickname, then a grin spread out over his face. "Why don't we go to my house and take these rules of yours for a test drive?"

Playing with fire. Wes was not the man she expected when she'd walked into his bookstore. She had a strange compulsion to peel back the layers and find out just who this man was.

Could she do that and keep her clothes on? Or maybe do it naked, but keep her emotions in check?

One way to find out. "Lead on, book boy."

Other Books by Jennifer Lyon

THE SAVAGED ILLUSIONS SERIES
Savaged Surrender, A Novella

THE PLUS ONE CHRONICLES TRILOGY
The Proposition (Book #1)
Possession (Book #2)
Obsession (Book #3)
The Plus One Chronicles Boxed Set

THE WING SLAYER HUNTER SERIES
Blood Magic (Book #1)
Soul Magic (Book #2)
Night Magic (Book #3)
Sinful Magic (Book #4)
Forbidden Magic (Book #4.5 a novella)
Caged Magic (Book #5)

Writing as Jennifer Apodaca

ONCE A MARINE SERIES
The Baby Bargain (Book #1)
Her Temporary Hero (Book #2)
Exposing The Heiress (Book #3)

About the Author

Jennifer Lyon is the pseudonym for *USA Today* Bestselling Author Jennifer Apodaca. Jen lives in Southern California where she continually plots ways to convince her husband that they should get a dog. After all, they met at the dog pound, fell in love, married and had three wonderful sons. So far, however, she has failed in her doggy endeavor. She consoles herself by pouring her passion into writing books. To date, Jen has published more than twenty books and novellas, won numerous awards and had her books translated into multiple languages, but she still hasn't come up with a way to persuade her husband that they need a dog.

Jen loves connecting with fans. Visit her website at www.jenniferlyonbooks.com or follow her at www.facebook.com/jenniferlyonbooks.

CPSIA information can be obtained
at www.ICGtesting.com
Printed in the USA
LVOW11s1834051017
551319LV00003B/654/P